The Island of Misfit Toys

BOUND TO EXCEL
Published by Bound to Excel
Elkhart, IN
www.boundtoexcel.com

ISBN 0-9763076-2-6

Printed in the United States of America

Cover design and layout by Alison L. King
Duesenberg art provided by Duke Edwards,
www.dukesdoodles.com

The Island of Misfit Toys

by André Swartley

For Kate—my toughest critic and my favorite audience.

Part I:

The Island of Misfit Toys

1

My father and my uncle died in a fantastic alcohol-fire explosion while working in the pit at the Kalamazoo Speedway. The event was televised, of course, and by the time I was four, Mom still had a recording of it buried at the bottom of her yarn basket in the living room. I found the tape one morning while she was out mowing the lawn.

I only saw a few seconds of footage: *There's Dad and Uncle Bobby poised at their places in the pit. The car rolls in. The driver is waving his arms back and forth, maybe signaling everyone to get the heck out of the way...*

BOOM! The two mechanics who lived through the blast are rolling in the grass, brushing frantically at their coveralls, although no one watching can see the invisible alcohol flames roasting off their skin.

I remember giggling at the men rolling in the grass like horses rolling in dirt on Channel 8 animal shows. But I didn't like what I had seen. For a few weeks after that, I checked on the tape every day at the bottom of the yarn basket, driven by the same instinct that made me check under my bed for monsters before going to sleep, but I never watched it again.

NASCAR had sponsored the event, but their lawyers bunged

up the liability contracts for all the pit workers. The organization ended up awarding one million dollars to the families of all six mechanics who were killed. Mom and Aunt Marguerite never had to work again.

Eleanor and I were three months old when it happened, almost to the day. Marguerite held me and took care of me just as often as Mom did. The same was true for Mom and Eleanor. We were a family.

2

Marguerite didn't even wait until Mom was out of the house. That's how Mom knew it wasn't an accident. Marguerite was feeding me. I was in her lap, eight months old, hunched the way only a baby can be hunched, gumming puréed squash off a plastic spoon. Mom was washing dishes. Eleanor lay in her portable bassinet in a chair scooted up to the Formica table. I know she was there because years later, when I was old enough to understand when people spoke, Marguerite whispered to me that Eleanor laughed and cooed when I hit the floor.

At first, there was no way to tell that Eleanor would not be a beautiful little girl. Her mother had gorgeous red hair falling in soft curls down past her shoulders and skin that made cream look rough. Eleanor took after her mother in every way, at least from the beginning.

But so did I. And then some.

I was outward perfection. Despite my mother's inconspicuous, straight-brown-haired attractiveness, I had dark red curls from the beginning. Clear green eyes like Marguerite's, but without the gold flecks, and skin out of a renaissance painting. I was so darn pretty, nobody suspected I was a boy, and when they found out, they were even more impressed.

Marguerite's hidden jealousy worked on Eleanor as surely as the years worked on Dorian Gray's portrait. Eleanor grew gaunt and bizarre, breaking out in so-called "baby acne" at five months, and never losing it. Exaggerated neck, nose, and ears; bulbous eyes with fleshy, camel-like lids; huge feet and hands along with bony wrists and ankles; adult teeth the same size as her baby teeth; glacial gums—need I go on?

"I'm not so sure he likes this food, Alice," Marguerite said. "He's squirming all over the place." Setting the stage.

"Here, I'm done with the dishes," Mom said, wiping her strong, thin hands on a dish towel. "I'll see if I can get him to—"

At this point, Mom told me, she heard a soft thump from behind her. The sound, she said, was horrible in its smallness.

Mom said Marguerite's eyes were so wide she could see white all around her beautiful gold-green irises. "He slipped…" Marguerite stammered. "I-I couldn't…he was just so wiggly."

Mom stood frozen with her back to the sink, hands holding her upright against the counter. I know I can't remember this, but I see her so clearly, right down to the wisps of straight brown hair illuminated by the sunlight pouring through the window behind her. She is beautiful in my mind. Beautiful in her horror.

My doctor said the first fall just dislocated my left shoulder, which gave me a mild, but supposedly permanent, hump in my back, just like Quasimodo. The real offense came next.

Marguerite reached down, still in her chair (that she didn't stand to pick me up bothers Mom nearly as much as the whole incident itself). I was squalling to high heaven, blood rushing through my body up to my damaged shoulder, preparing a bruise that would last over a month. She picked me up in the beautiful hands her own daughter would never have, raised my body about three feet off the floor, and dropped me again, upside down. I stopped crying instantly, according to my mother, and I didn't say a word for nearly five years.

3

The morning Kindergarten teacher at Auburn Elementary, Miss Felicia Aloe ("AL-A-*WAY*," she shouted at us the first day of class, grinning and terrified at teaching a class for the first time), decided my first day that I would have no responsibilities.

I appeared at the door with my hand attached to my mother's in a first-day-of-school death grip. So far so good.

Miss Aloe baby-stepped toward us like a tennis player loading up for a forehand, her hand thrust downward as far in front of her as possible, presumably to shake my hand.

Her eyes flicked upward. One horrified glance at my lumpy head and maniacal red hair set off her silent alarm that I was SPECIAL ED (Mom's note from Dr. Hyrnewyc claiming I had a speaking disorder called "Selective Aphasia" didn't help); suddenly her main job concerning me was to keep me from mauling the other students.

She bared her teeth in what I soon learned was her attempt at cheerful comfort, as if a voice in her head was telling her, *Keep grinning, Felicia, whatever you do.*

It was sadder for her than for me, actually; her hopes for a stellar rookie year of teaching were dashed, and all it took was me walking into her room. All she had ever wanted was to help children learn to read, and she had to get hired at a school that supports the classroom inclusion of—

"GOOD MORNING, YOUNG MAN. WHAT'S YOUR NAME?"

I obviously couldn't answer. Mom shook Miss Aloe's hand and saved the day. "Clifford Carlson." Then Mom made things worse again by proving I was smart: "That's an alliterative name, right honey?" She patted my head. I nodded.

This time Miss Aloe's inner voice was nearly audible: *Dear God.* "WELCOME TO KINDERGARTEN, CLIFFORD CARLSON," she wailed.

Mom snapped a picture.

Miss Aloe began immediately to make me different. She beamed at me a lot, and spoke slowly through her white, always-smiling teeth. The cords in her neck stood out like pencils under her skin. "DO YOU WANT SOME CRACKERS WHILE THE OTHER STUDENTS DO LEVEL TESTS?" she said to me that first day after my mom left. Throughout that first semester, sometimes it was cookies, sometimes apple slices. The other kids learned quickly that talking to me was a NO-NO.

Christmas break was wonderful because my mother read to me in the mornings and helped me write simple responses about whether I liked the books in the afternoon. She let me watch TV for one hour in the evening.

I remember watching *Christmas Vacation* because it was one of the few times Mom let me stay up late. We sat on the couch together, me resting my lopsided head in the crevice between Mom's arm and her right breast, my already odd hair standing up with static from snuggling against Mom's sweater. Mom had loved Chevy Chase ever since she had watched him fall off the Oval Office desk while decorating a Christmas tree on the first season Saturday Night Live. But *Christmas Vacation* wasn't her favorite movie until after I spoke my first words.

***

My first day back in Kindergarten after the break was also my last. The other kids were used to me by now. They weren't mean, but they ignored me. I don't blame them; like I said, Miss Aloe made sure I was always doing something different, just in case I would go crazy and attack another kid with my safety pencil, I guess. The other students were drawing messy pictures of their favorite Christmas presents. I had started drawing with a colored pencil, which Miss Aloe yanked from my hand, and replaced with a hunk of yellow cheese. "NO, CLIFFORD, THESE ARE TOO DANGEROUS," she said, shaking the colored pencil in front of my eyes. "OWIE. COME SIT HERE AND EAT YOUR SNACK."

She dropped said pencil when a new little girl with poofy, hairsprayed blonde hair pointed at me and said, "What's wrong with your head? Are you a troglodyte?"

Lord knows where she picked up this word, but she wasn't the only one handing out surprises; I opened my mouth and echoed Randy Quaid from *Christmas Vacation*: "My hair just ain't gonna look right."

I'm not sure who was more surprised—Miss Aloe, the other kids, or me. Alford Milner, who sometimes gave me Chips Ahoy from his lunch when Miss Aloe wasn't looking, clapped. Agnes Young, on whom I had a desperate crush, said, "Cliff, you talked!" I just stood there with my mouth open, unable to move.

Miss Aloe seemed to take my speech as a threat; she marched me down to the office, beaming gruesomely into open classrooms as we passed by. Her heels clicked loudly in the hallway, a very businesslike sound.

In the main office, she sat me down in a padded chair and disappeared into the principal's office. Wordless shrieks came from behind the principal's closed door—apparently Miss Aloe's fear of me had reached its breaking point. I imagined her holding her face in her hands, shaking, while the principal offered awkward comfort in the form of a few pats on the back.

She came out after several minutes. Her puffy eyes were smeared all around with black eye shadow and mascara. She announced, inches from my face, "YOU CAN LEARN FROM YOUR MOMMY AT HOME NOW." I could have hugged her right then, but the shock probably would've killed her.

4

Mom and I had shared written notes at the dinner table and at bedtime since I was four. I wasn't writing novels or anything, but I could write *Thank you for dinner, I love you,* and *You are a good mommy* before I was five. I adored my mother so much I didn't need to express anything else.

That last day of school I showed up on our front porch at ten in the morning, bearing a good-luck granola bar from Miss Aloe and a note I'd written with her help: *They sent me home. I'm dangerous.* Mom called the school and bawled out everyone she spoke to until the principal himself got on the line. He told her I had verbally threatened another student at school, and Mom squealed into the phone, "My baby talked! What'd he say?" When she heard the answer she slammed the phone so hard in its cradle that the whole thing fell off the wall and cracked its housing on the same floor that had cracked my head four-and-a-half years earlier. Neither of us even noticed until later; Mom was making too much noise, carrying on about how she had the smartest little boy in the world and swinging me around in her arms.

Compared to that moment, I try to imagine what a life-sucking disappointment it must have been when she found out I couldn't speak like a normal person. The realization came almost immediately. "What else do you have to say, honey?" she asked. Her voice sounded casual, but with violent bubbles of laughter behind it. She had waited so long.

I tried to say my favorite note that I wrote her at least once a day. Instead of "You are a good mommy," my voice, on its virgin voyage in my home, offered this: "A meal in itself." I assume it came from the Campbell's soup commercial tagline.

Mom's mouth was open wide, prepared for the aforementioned laugh to come tumbling out, but she only managed a little squeak. "What does that mean, honey?" she asked after a moment.

I touched my thumb and forefinger together and twirled them in the air, requesting a pen and paper.

Any trace of Mom's laugh, or even a smile, were gone now. She grabbed my shoulders. Her nails dug through my sweatshirt. "You are *done* writing down everything. You can say what you want now. Just say the word and you can have anything you want." Her eyes were huge. "Say something!" She shook me like a bad mom on TV.

She let go of me and sat back on the kitchen floor. "Oh God," she whispered to the linoleum. "I'm sorry."

I didn't know if she was apologizing to God or to me, but I hugged as far around her shoulders as I could reach. Eventually her hands, gentle again, clasped my forearm. "I'm sorry, baby," she repeated.

♪

The greatest thing Eleanor ever did for me was lie to me about my name. My parents named me Clifford Robert Carlson, after my mother's father, and called me Cliff. I was six, and no longer suffering Miss Aloe's Kindergarten class, when she told me the "truth" about my grandfather's—and consequently *my*—name.

"The army made him shorten it because it wouldn't fit on the draft card," she whispered. She flipped up the collar of the new denim jacket she'd received for Christmas and threw furtive glances around our living room, as if she were sharing matters of national security. "My mom and your mom fought over who would get Pappy's big important name for her kid. But since I was a girl your mom got to use the name." Here she snorted loudly, a sound like a chorus of migrating geese. I believed then that sound came out of her jealousy. Now I think she was just trying not to laugh.

I was practically humming with anticipation. *Tell me the name!* my mind shrieked at her. Not so much as a whisper came out my mouth, of course; I didn't want to say anything weird that would make her not tell.

Suddenly Eleanor grabbed my cheeks and jaw. "Make a sound," she commanded. "Anything. Whine like you normally

do. I don't care." She forced my mouth into the correct shapes
while slowly enunciating the name along with me.

In just under a month of this exercise, Eleanor, a six-year-
old child, managed something no one else would ever do: she
discovered my voice. Sure, I had spoken nonsense before I got
out this whopper of a name, but nothing purposeful. My only
regret was that I didn't get to use my name at Kindergarten—
Miss Aloe would've had a wonderful fit hearing it.

Still, "What's your name?" is a pretty standard question,
and even after I found out Eleanor had lied, I spoke the lie with
confidence every time someone asked. Better than Pavlov and
his drooling dogs. Instead of dog food, however, my incentive
was hearing Eleanor repeat, over and over, "Oh, your mom will
be so proud."

She cried at our last rehearsal. She coughed and honked out
her huge nose to cover her tears. For that one instant, I believe,
she was proud of me and proud of herself, which I know was
a rarity for her. She even hugged me. I can still feel her hard,
greasy cheek on my neck, and hear her shrill whisper: "You did
great."

The next week her spirits were back to normal. She made me
eavesdrop on my mother telling Marguerite what I had told a
lady at the grocery store who had asked my name.

"You're dumber than brass balls," Eleanor told me. "I made
that whole thing up." Her narrow, pale tongue flicked over her
miniature teeth. "What an idiot." But she patted my back,
purposely avoiding my disfigured shoulder, which she knew still
caused me a good deal of pain at the slightest touch. "A real
idiot."

My mother *was* proud, though. I could hear it in her voice
as she called me out to the kitchen to display my new skill to
her sister. So when she asked what I had told that nice lady
at the store my name was, I answered, without stutter or flaw,
"Heathcliffton Marybob Carlsonipschidt."

6

Christmas television proved again to be life-changing the next year—1991, I think. For the first time since the drop, Mom invited Marguerite and Eleanor to the house for Christmas. I don't even guess at Marguerite's motivation for accepting. I like to think the two sisters, best friends for so many years, just missed each other.

Eleanor lay on the floor, bathed in the blue light of the TV, adorned in the now omnipresent denim jacket. I had only asked her about it once—in the form of a note, of course. Her casual response, "Mom says the thicker fabric keeps me from looking too bony," kept me silent about the denim jackets from then on. Even in summer, when sweat rolled from her forehead down her pointed nose and dripped onto whatever surface was just below her: sidewalk, living room rug, coloring book. She was vampirically pale, with thick red lips and red-rimmed eyes. In the winter months, blue was the only color which flattered her; all yellows, greens, and reds made her *skin* appear blue, as if she were constantly suffering hypothermia. I'm pleased to say Eleanor prettied up in the summers; the sun bleached her strawberry hair and tanned her skin. Nobody would have called her cute, but she looked healthy at least.

Now, though, in the middle of winter: vampire. Colored pencils were scattered all around her and the one-dollar Christmas coloring book from Wal Mart my mom kept in the house. Even at six she couldn't keep her marks inside the lines. Jagged spikes of color leapt back and forth across the drawn lines on her page like meaty football players bickering at the line of scrimmage.

We were trying to watch *Rudolph the Red Nosed Reindeer*, but the news had already broken into the prime time children's programming twice. Peter Jennings wanted to tell us about the troops in Iraq, and how they were celebrating Christmas in huge sandy tents, thousands of miles from home. All this intermixed with phosphorescent green and black shots of Baghdad getting blasted by our Air Force.

With each bombardment, each picture of soldiers glaring at their imported turkey, our family room grew chillier. That my father, whose parents had emigrated from Canada before he could walk, had registered as a Conscientious Objector, while Uncle Bobby had packed up for Boot Camp and served his two years right out of high school, had always been a sore spot for Marguerite. She dared not say anything about Dad—she was too enamored with having Mom to pal around with again—but she associated pacifism with America's neighbor to the north, and will be a Canada basher to the end.

Peter Jennings (who, thankfully, Marguerite did not know was Canadian, or she would have changed the channel, thereby causing me to miss my favorite part of *Rudolph*, where the terrifying Bumble caps Santa's huge Christmas tree with a golden star) promised more details as they arose, and sent us back to *Rudolph*. The claymation lion, wearing a crown and angelic wings, was describing the Island of Misfit toys to Yukon Cornelius, Rudolph, and Herbie on the screen.

"Misfit island, huh?" Marguerite said. "Where's that? Prince Edward Island?" She snorted at her own joke.

Mom held her tongue.

"Where's that, Mommy?" Eleanor looked up from the ruined Santa Claus she was coloring.

"That's where people go when they can't take the responsibilities of the real world." She tapped her finger lightly on Eleanor's huge beak.

"I'm having some tea," Mom said. Her knuckles were white on the arms of her chair as she stood.

"Freaks go there," Marguerite whispered.

Eleanor flipped up the stiff collar of her jacket and bared her tiny teeth at me, increasing the Count Dracula resemblance tenfold.

I didn't care. There was a place for people who don't fit in with everyone else. People who write their words down instead of speaking, perhaps? People who, when they do speak, just repeat stuff they have heard on TV, or in songs, or read in books, perhaps?

"Bibbity-bobbity-boo," I whispered.

Part 2:

Cliff

1

Mom's back started giving her trouble the summer I turned sixteen. She blamed the pain on years of being overprotective and hauling me around on one arm when I could have walked anywhere I wanted.

The pain was most evident during my weekly haircuts, when she had to bend over for twenty minutes at a shot. Ever since my first haircut when I was four (I stayed bald for three years after Marguerite dropped me), Mom had realized a hairbrush wouldn't hurt my lumpy head after all, and she could wage an all-out war on each of my bizarre cowlicks every seven days if she wanted.

"It's time you go to a real barber," she declared abruptly one Saturday. I was already straddling a kitchen chair with my shirt off, an old bed sheet around my shoulders. She smiled, but there was a tightness around her eyes that had never been there before.

I shrugged back into my t-shirt, slung an arm around her shoulders, and steered her toward the garage. I had noticed the way she hissed through clenched teeth every time she bent over or straightened up for a couple months now.

***

A sign by the cash register said the salon charged thirteen dollars for a male haircut and a shampoo. The poster showed a handsome, smiling man with his head tilted into a sleek black sink, and his hair lost in two tidy hemispheres of white suds. "Oh, he's got some muscle problems in his neck," Mom said immediately to the stylist. "The shampooing might hurt him."

Mom! I gave her an outraged look. Girls already thought I was strange enough when I saw them in town and wouldn't say a word for fear of emitting some Turrets-like outburst. *I'll be fine,* the look said. *Go sit down.*

She put her hands up. *Fine, fine, I'll stop helping you and being a good mother.* After fifteen years our nonverbal communication bordered on telepathy.

"Tell you what," the girl said, "We'll put some towels down by your neck so you won't have to lean so far." She smiled. The three silver rings in her bottom lip glinted in the salon's ultraviolet lighting.

I smiled back nervously and gave her the thumbs-up. Mom pursed her lips, but sat down quietly in the chair beside me and pulled a magazine off the counter.

"You don't talk much, do you?"

I stared in the mirror at her inky-black hair and wondered if those spikes would draw blood from my finger if I touched them.

"His name is Cliff," Mom said. "He's very smart, but he isn't wired for talking." She flipped a page in her magazine. "He loves haircuts."

Normally at this speech—especially the "he's very smart" part—the listener would get weird and start talking loudly and slowly, like I didn't understand the language. The girl surprised me. "Cliff, huh?" she said, folding up towels to put around my neck. "Well I love haircuts too, but it's because I get to use scissors on a fellow human being. Lean back."

She had a little hose with a showerhead on it, and she sprayed it into her cupped palm to test the water's temperature. "First time at a barber?" she asked. "You look terrified."

"Stretch out with your *feelings!*" I said.

A pause. "I'm sorry?"

"Obiwan Kenobi," Mom said, still not looking up from her magazine.

"Oh. Awesome."

I thought I heard my mom snort laughter into her magazine, but with my head in the sink the rush of water overpowered most other sounds. Then she turned the spray on my head. My expression must have changed because she said, "Not bad, huh?" Her smile was almost a smirk, but still kind. "Wait 'til I rub in the shampoo."

Twenty-five minutes later my hair stood up at sharp angles from my scalp, but, for the first time ever, on purpose. Mom said I looked hip. The girl agreed. "Oh yeah. Totally." She had a dry way of speaking, like she was constantly making fun of something, but I didn't think it was me or my mom.

At the register Mom said, "I've always tried to get his hair to lay flat. I never thought of trying to make it stick up."

"The wheels are always turning under this minefield of metal and mousse." She pointed to her head.

"Yes, well," Mom said. She handed the girl a twenty-dollar bill. "Keep it."

The girl lost her smirk. "Thank you."

"Who can we request the next time Cliff needs a cut?"

"Bethany," she said. "I'm always here."

2

Mom gave me jobs and an allowance toward a car when I got my driver's license. The neighbors shook their heads and *tsk*-ed whenever Mom set me to mowing the lawn, shoveling the drive, or pulling weeds; she told me Edith Clemens across the street had called her once and asked her if I was really up to manual labor with my condition. I could tell Mom enjoyed reliving the tongue-lashing she gave Edith Clemens from the way her eyes sparkled.

"No one else in the neighborhood called my parenting into question again. At least not to my face."

I wrote, *Tyrant.*

The truth was I loved doing those chores. Once I built up some muscle, the hump all but left my shoulder, and the pain I'd suffered there my whole life went with it.

One morning in early September while we were in the garden together she sat back on her haunches and blew her sweaty hair out of her eyes. Her wrists hung limply over her thighs, gloved hands looking large and clownish. "I think you've just about worked off a good down payment."

My jaw must have landed in the tomato plants but Mom

pretended not to notice. She peeled off her gloves. "Why don't we shower up and go shopping."

I took off for the house at a dead sprint before she could change her mind.

The closest dealerships to Auburn are in Fort Wayne. Talk about irony: the Auburn Cord Duesenberg Museum in Auburn is in the restored showroom of the old Auburn factory, where they made some of the most luxurious and expensive cars in the world in the early Twentieth Century, and we had to drive thirty minutes if we wanted to buy a Geo Metro.

I didn't buy a Geo Metro. I bought (well, okay, *Mom* bought the car, but we both agreed that I earned it) the most beautiful Toyota Corolla ever made. Mom had feared any type of sports car since Dad died, so I think this was, in her mind, the antithesis of sports cars.

Who cares! It was my first set of wheels. My first ride. I suppose many sixteen-year-old boys wouldn't be so excited about a beige Corolla, and I understand that. But for the next two years I washed that car every Saturday (assuming the water didn't freeze on its way out of the hose, as sometimes happened in the winter) and wiped down the dash and steering wheel with Armor All. I worked my tail off at home in lieu of monthly payments; Mom paid off the car right away, but, like she said, I had only worked off a down payment. She would let me know when I was out of her debt.

3

The first time I drove myself to the salon I made Bethany come outside to see the Corolla. She seemed surprised when I dragged her out of the salon by her hand (she had only been cutting my hair for a few months), but besides Mom, who saw the car everyday, Bethany was my only friend. I had to show *someone*.

I stood nearly in the middle of Main Street with my arms out wide, showcasing the beige Corolla. *Ta-DAH!*

Bethany, bless her, put a hand to her mouth and worked very hard not to laugh. When she had herself under control she said, "Yours?"

I slapped a hand to my chest and nodded. *Yes. Mine.* "Welcome to the Buddy Ebsen society," I said.

That set her off for good. She crumpled right there in the street and shook with silent, breathless laughter until I thought she would pass out. I tried to play hurt, but it felt so good to laugh with someone, I sat down and joined her.

I wrote her a quick note. *If you aren't careful all this laughing will tear out your lip rings.* That only made things worse. I had to drag her to the sidewalk, where she eventually got up, alternating between heavy coughing and high sighs of amusement.

"You are about the coolest guy I know, Cliff," she said, sitting on the curb. "How would you like to see my car?"

Of course I wanted to see her car. "The mummy's after us. Walk faster," I said.

"We'll go right after your haircut."

"Okay, it's not mine, but I wish it was."

I could see why. "Her" car was stuffed back into a corner of her father's museum: a black 1937 Cord Phaeton Coupe, polished to a gleam. High molded fenders over whitewall tires; bright silver hoses trailing from the driver's side of the engine compartment; tall black grill with a silver angel at its peak, its wings folded back in the illusion of flying at great speed. This car could *eat* my beige Corolla and crap it out the tailpipe as scrap metal.

"*Just* a bit outside," I breathed.

"I know. It's amazing." Bethany gestured behind her. "The rest of the cars in here I could take or leave, but don't tell my dad I said that."

I wouldn't be telling her dad *anything* coherent in the foreseeable future and we both knew it, but I took what she said at face value and shook my head.

"I grew up around these cars," she continued, pulling me away from the Cord. "Since Dad never had a son to man around with, he decided I would have to do." The soles of her boots clapped and echoed on the showroom's polished tile floor.

"Look at this Model J." She grabbed my hand and pulled me over to the open driver's window of a blue and black Duesenberg. There were small tears here and there in the leather bench seat, but for the most part the interior gleamed as brightly as the outside. "Dad's had me driving and parking most of these cars since I could reach the pedals, which I take to mean he loves me. You can really screw up an engine if you don't know what you're doing." I could see she was warming up. "That little metal knob on the steering wheel lets you decide when sparkplugs fire in the pistons' rotation. You drive around and do the wrong thing to that knob, best case you stall the engine, worst case, kiss your Duesy goodbye."

She still had my hand. "I bet you a dollar no other girl in Auburn knows how to advance the spark in a 1935 Duesenberg."

Strange thing to bet on, but I wouldn't have disagreed if I could have; I was too focused on her fingers laced through mine. We started walking again. Or, to be more accurate, she started towing me around again. At this point I could not have moved under my own power to escape all the bears in Alaska—not while touching a girl for the first time in my life. "Of course, Dad has never let me drive that one. One of three made in '35 with a supercharged Straight Eight and leather top. Retailed for over fifteen thousand dollars when a Ford or Chevy cost less than five hundred. This was a car you bought if you wanted to be noticed."

4

Exactly two weeks from my eighteenth birthday, we found out "being overprotective" was not the reason for my mother's back pain. Mom's X-rays were on a lighted board on the wall in front of us. The bottom half of her spine appeared dim compared to the other luminous bones in the picture. I pulled out my pad and pen. *Bone cancer?* I wrote.

"No, and for that at least we can be grateful; the pain would be much worse. No, your mother had several conspicuous moles on her torso, which, as you know, we have removed and tested."

Mom and Marguerite had been good NASCAR wives; they came to every race my dad and uncle worked in wearing halter tops and no sunscreen. As long as you're outside, you might as well get a tan, right?

"Certain cancer cells grow in certain parts of your body, then those same cells go ruin other body parts too," Dr. Hyrnewyc explained. He had diagnosed my shoulder hump as permanent seventeen years ago, and I decided he must be wrong about this as well. "In your mother's case, skin cancer cells have moved into her bones. The cancer has bored its way through the bone here." Dr. Hyrnewyc drew his finger across the X-ray of Mom's lumbar. "The bone is much more porous now, and becoming brittle."

"My back pain," Mom said. Her voice was calm.

The doctor nodded and folded his hands in a fig leaf over his fly.

I breathed deeply and waited for him to get to the part that began with, *The good news is...*

"Skin cancer is treatable, like many cancers, in its early stages."

I willed him to say it: *The good news is...*

"However." The word was a sentence in every way possible. "Even though we've removed each of the melanomas, they've still had a few years to do their work. In addition to your bones, Mrs. Carlson, the cancer has metastasized to the pancreas. And your recent headaches indicate it may have moved to the brain as well."

I didn't listen. *When can Mom come home?*

Dr. Hyrnewyc read the note and glanced at my mother. He answered slowly, "I'm sorry, Cliff, your mother's going to have to stay here for now."

Mom took my hand and squeezed it until my knuckles cracked, but her voice was still calm. "You can visit me whenever you want."

The doctor stirred, perhaps to inform me of the visiting hours, but then seemed to think better of it. He nodded and stepped out without a word.

♪

The sun was high and warm, filling our house with comforting yellow light when Marguerite and Eleanor moved in. At first they only brought a couple suitcases each. I had to leave the hospital to unlock the house for them.

I handed Marguerite a note. *Your house key is on the table. Do you need anything else? I would like to get back to Mom.*

Eleanor read over her shoulder. "You're not letting Cliff leave are you?" she whined, her cheeks shiny and flushed above the blue collar of her jean jacket. "Why does he get to leave when I have to stay here and—"

She broke off at her mother's glare. But only for a second. "I bet he's not even going to the hospital. I bet he's going to visit that whore of a girlfr—"

"Eleanor, shut up. I will not see you again until your suitcase is unpacked and your new room is clean."

Eleanor fled.

Marguerite spared me her wrath. "Of course, Cliff. Tell your mother we'll be over this evening."

Eleanor was half correct about me seeing Bethany. I picked her up at her house so she could visit Mom with me. Her father met me at the door. "Hello, Cliff."

I had written the note ahead of time. *Hello Mr. Wray. How are preparations for the auto show going?*

"Fine, fine. I'm taking the '35 Model J and I promised Allain he could drive the speedster this year," he said wistfully. The speedster was a yellow Auburn convertible coupe with a duck-tail trunk. In the museum it rested on an elevated turntable. Just like the '37 Cord was Bethany's pick of the litter, the speedster was Mr. Wray's.

Finally getting rid of your old clunkers? Good for you.

"Clunkers! That's a good one." He stepped aside to let me in. "Each of those 'clunkers' is worth more than all the houses on this block, if I were selling." He balled up the note and pitched it into the trashcan in the kitchen. "No, I wouldn't have anything to brag about if I got rid of either of those cars. I'm just showing them."

Good luck.

"Well thank you. You ought to come up with me." Then he remembered where Bethany and I were going tonight, and that I probably wouldn't be spending a weekend away from town anytime soon. "Sometime," he amended.

"If Cliff wanted to be bored to death he wouldn't need to go to the auto show," Bethany said, coming from the hallway into the kitchen. "Your museum is just down the road."

"You don't mean that. That's your teen angst talking."

"Dad, I'm twenty-five."

"I love you, Bethany. I know you don't mean all the terrible things you say to me."

"What a weirdo," Bethany said as we stepped out the front door.

Your dad rocks.

She glanced down at the note. "I know."

Marguerite was already in Mom's room when we got there. *That was fast*, I wrote to Bethany. She didn't even read the note;

she just stared hard at Marguerite. She hadn't had the years to forgive her that I did.

"Hi honey." I had been watching Bethany so closely—in case she leapt at Marguerite, glossy black fingernails raised—I hadn't even looked at Mom yet. The sadness in her voice, though, made me forget everyone in the room besides her.

I pushed past Marguerite. Vaguely, I noticed her stuffing an envelope into her purse.

Mom cupped my cheek in her palm. "Hi baby," she said again, and her hand fell back to her side.

She was stalling. I picked up the fallen hand and squeezed gently. *What is it?*

Her eyes flicked over to Marguerite, and back to me. *I'm sorry.* The message couldn't have been clearer if she'd spoken aloud.

I recoiled, as if from a beloved pet gone rabid. Suddenly the envelope I'd seen in Marguerite's purse didn't seem so unimportant.

Marguerite seized the opening. "I have to get this to our lawyer before the office closes. I'll see you tomorrow, Alice. Cliff." She looked Bethany right in the eye, then left without another word.

I still sat on the side of Mom's bed, but I felt a cold gap growing between us. I felt like I was seeing her through the wrong end of a telescope.

"They gave me two weeks, Cliff."

Further apart now—Mom and I were on two bare mountain peaks separated by a valley hidden under clouds.

"Your aunt can take good care of you."

My fingertips and teeth tingled like they were asleep.

"She and Eleanor will be with you now. Like before." Mom's voice broke on *before*. "We're—you're a family."

Stop talking. My head hurt. The hair on the sides of my head was bunched up in my fists.

Mom was dying.

Two weeks.

What was the rest?

I rocked back and forth on the bed, my eyes squeezed shut, my fists still clenching my hair, now beating against my ears from the outside like my heartbeat did from the inside.

"*Clifford Robert.*"

All the sadness was gone from Mom's face. Our two mountain peaks crashed back together and we were on the hospital bed again, two feet apart.

"I'm not dead yet," she said. "Anyway, what do doctors know? They said you'd never talk."

"Nice beaver," I agreed.

Mom's mouth twitched up, and she laughed like wedding bells. For a moment the IV in her hand and the pale hospital gown had no power over her; she was beautiful and healthy again.

But only for a moment. "Cliff, I'm sorry I didn't tell you about Marge and Eleanor moving in. I didn't want you to worry about it. And Marge has grown so much. I don't want to die without seeing my son and my sister build a relationship."

She turned to Bethany, who still faced the door, her mouth a grim line. "Bethany, Marge just doesn't understand you. She doesn't see how you are with Cliff, how wonderful you can be." Clouds seemed to be pouring from Bethany's head and warring with the UV lights in the room. Mom had never spoken down to Bethany before, and certainly not to me; she'd spent her entire motherhood working against that very thing.

"I know," Bethany finally said. "I'm everything she's not: ugly and nice."

"Excuse me?" Mom said, rising up out of her bed. Harsh, irregular blotches of red rose in her cheeks and forehead.

"No, excuse me," Bethany said. "I need some air." She left without waiting for a response from Mom or me.

"She can't say those things about my sister," Mom said. She still sat ramrod straight in the bed. "She can't."

I brought up my notepad. *Mom, M and E hate Bethany, and you know it. M didn't even say hello or goodbye to her. E called her a whore before I left home. Bethany is the only person besides you who is nice to me.*

Mom lay back in the bed when she read the note. She wouldn't look at me. "That girl won't break up the only family I have left. Not now."

We were back on our mountains. Mom had never talked like this before in her life. Family? *I* was her family, and she was mine.

What was that paper that Marguerite had in her purse?

Mom took the note. "Cliff, honey, I'm very tired." She closed her eyes and turned her head sideways on the pillow. A tear rolled down her cheek and made a dark spot on the pillow. "Cliff?" she said, still facing away. "The car is yours now. You're done paying for it." Finally she turned back. "I'll see you tomorrow, okay?"

If I had known I would never see her again, I doubt I would have let her dismiss me like that. I like to think we could have worked things out. At least I could have written her one of my notes: *You're the best mom in the world.*

I love you.

But who knows? Neither of us was listening very well.

6

I found Bethany in the parking lot, leaning against the beige Corolla, hands in her pockets, eyes closed. The sun had disappeared with morning, and now clouds hung over us like the pendulous belly of a great cat.

I wanted so badly to apologize to her. To explain—even though she knew as well as I—that the things Mom had said to her came from the cancer, not from her own mouth. *People say all sorts of silly things when they're sick*, I wanted to say. *Mom loves you almost as much as I do. Did you hear that?* I would have shouted, if I could. *I love you!*

Of course, I couldn't. "I like to keep the kitchen tidy," I told her instead.

She didn't even answer. Her hands stayed in her pockets, her eyes stayed closed.

Never before had I felt so impotent. I turned up to the gray sky and made the only declaration I could control, and I made it loudly: "HEATHCLIFFTON MARYBOB CARLSONIPSCHIDT!"

I raged at the low clouds, broadcasting my dominion over the spoken word: "HEATHCLIFFTON MARYBOB CARLSONIPSCHIDT!"

The beige Corolla caught my wrath next. I kicked a tire.

"HEATHCLIFFTON MARYBOB CARLSONIPSCHIDT!"   I kicked again, savagely. The plastic hubcap broke.

"Cliff, those hubcaps are like forty bucks apiece at the dealership." Bethany's eyes were still closed. She must have heard the plastic crack. "C'mere."

Her calmness, more than anything else, ended my tantrum. Slowly she pulled her hands out of her pockets and wrapped her arms around my waist. My chin came down on the top of her head. Her hair was hard and spiky, like I'd imagined, but the spikes bowed to my skin instead of pricking.

"I know what it's like to lose a mother, Cliff. And I can't imagine what it would be like to lose both parents—I keep myself awake at night sometimes thinking about what I would do if Dad died...I will not leave you, Cliff." She pulled back and her eyes were wet. "Listen to me: I will not leave you."

I believed her. And what's more, she believed herself.

7

Bethany wisely asked me to take her home when we left the hospital; supper was a grim affair in the Carlson household that night. I smelled hot dogs cooking on our George Foreman grill. Eleanor had gotten to pick the meal then. Probably a peace offering from Marguerite for yelling at her this afternoon.

"What's up *Clifford?*" Eleanor asked. My name always sounded like a swear word coming from her. Her jacket cuffs were unbuttoned and rolled up almost to her elbows while she cooked. She pointed a plastic spatula at me, which she was using to tend the dogs. "Where's your Goth goddess? Didn't feel like..." she trailed off and twirled the spatula around restlessly. Maybe she decided there wasn't much sport in tormenting someone whose mother was dying.

I hung my keys on the hook Mom had set up for me before she went to the hospital.

"Supper will be ready in a few minutes. I set the table," she said.

I smiled as well as I could and gave her a thumbs-up. *Good work*.

"How's Aunt Alice?" she asked. She looked very vulnerable, caring so much and trying not to care at the same time.

I shook my head. Thumbs-down.

"I'm sorry," she whispered. "Aunt Alice is tough, though. Just like that big fat head of yours."

I rapped on the side of my head with my knuckles. *Hard as a rock.*

Fear and canine adoration suddenly flashed across Eleanor's face and she whipped around to the George Foreman grill: a telltale sign that Marguerite was here even without icy psychological breeze that blew wherever she went. I heard her close the back door—I must have left it open.

"Is Alice resting, Cliff?"

I nodded.

"She looked tired today. That's a tough choice to make."

I frowned a question at her: What's *a tough choice to make?*

"Thank you for setting the table Eleanor."

"The hot dogs are done," Eleanor said, beaming at the praise.

"Did you toast the buns?"

Eleanor's face fell into a caricature of horror, except she wasn't pretending. A sitcom director would have cranked the laugh track at her expression.

No part of me laughed, inside or out. I waved a hand at Eleanor and scrunched up my nose. I hoped the gesture said, *Forget about it. Toasted buns are gross.* Anything to get that look off her face.

Marguerite shrugged too, but not to make Eleanor feel better. Her gesture conveyed that she had suspected as much, and what could she hope for besides untoasted buns for her hot dogs with a daughter like hers?

I wish I were exaggerating all this but I remember this last hour in Auburn with grotesque clarity, right down to the yellow and pink Easter napkins Eleanor had folded into clumsy triangles on our plates.

I reached for Eleanor's spatula, offering to help her get the food to the table. She yanked it out of my reach. *"What, Clifford?"* she yelled. Nearly eighteen years of hurt and embarrassment were suddenly unleashed, and Eleanor was their vehicle. "You don't trust me to scrape hot dogs off a fucking indoor grill?" Even Marguerite backed away with me, step for step. "You could do it better, right? I know you could, *Clifford!*" Tendons stood out in the hand holding the spatula. Her eyes bulged. Her wheezing was the only sound in the kitchen. In the *world*. The universe breathed with Eleanor.

If Marguerite hadn't spoken I probably wouldn't have driven halfway across the country, and I would have been sleeping in a room with padded walls by the end of the week.

"Eleanor, sweetheart, let Cliff help you."

Such a ridiculous hope shone in Eleanor's eyes at the word "sweetheart" that I felt like screaming. It was like watching one of those old Saturday matinees where a young girl walks into a closet where the audience knows a werewolf or vampire is hiding. *Don't go in there, Eleanor! She doesn't mean it! She's a* monster!

Eleanor figured it out on her own. She raised the spatula again and smiled impishly at her mother, then me. "Clifford," she said. Now she was the monster and I was the little kid in the closet. "You know what your mother did today?"

"Eleanor, you shut your mouth this instant." All traces of "sweetheart" were gone.

"She made Mother your legal guardian," Eleanor said dreamily. "We're like brother and sister now."

"Eleanor, don't you say anoth—"

There was a wet smack as Eleanor lashed out with the spatula. A bright red welt surfaced on Marguerite's perfect cheek, complete with white lines matching the pattern of holes on the spatula. Bits of charred hot dog hung on her skin.

"I'm talking now, *Mother*." Eleanor turned back to me, wearing the same smile as before. "Of course we won't be brother and sister for long, will we Mother?"

Marguerite held her cheek in one hand and did not answer.

Eleanor didn't seem to notice. "No, you'll be packaged up in a nice white jacket and shipped off to Terra Haute the day Aunt Alice dies, unable to speak, mad with grief over the death of the only woman who ever loved you." Her eyes grew wide and startled. "You attacked me, Clifford," she said. Her voice was suddenly a gross mockery of a child's. "And Mommy too." She backed away toward the counter. "You attacked us with a knife." She dropped the spatula and slowly opened a drawer. "No, Cliff." The pitch of her voice was rising. "Cliff, don't! Please!" In one quick motion she drew Mom's long J.A. Henckels utility knife from the drawer and set it to her arm.

I waited to see no more. I spun around and grabbed at the wall where my keys should have been. The hook was empty.

A jingling sound came from behind me. I imagined Eleanor's red lips and her many small teeth smiling at me while she held the knife in one hand and the keys in the other, shaking them between two fingers. In my mind's eye blood dripped from the keys onto the bright linoleum that had broken my own body so long ago.

I didn't turn around. I opened the door and I ran.

8

I had thought I was calm until Bethany opened the door and saw my expression. "Cliff, what's going on?" She sounded more worried than I felt.

I grasped at my pockets but I'd left my pad of paper in my car. "Yes, have some!" It even sounded like Rick Moranis in my head. I balled up my fist and pounded my thigh.

"It's okay, there's paper by the phone." One hand held the top of her robe closed, but her bare legs flashed from under it as I followed her to the kitchen.

She handed me a pen and read aloud as I wrote: "'Paper in M's purse at the hospital makes her...'" she paused. "'Makes her my legal guardian.' You have got to be kidding."

I tapped the paper with my pen. *Focus.*

"'E said they will send me to Terra Haute when Mom dies. She said they'll tell them...'"

A vision of Eleanor surfaced in my mind again, the all-purpose knife carving a wide red mouth in her forearm.

"Tell who? What's in Terra Haute? Cliff, I don't understand."

The adrenaline rush was beginning to fade. I set the pen hard to the page so my hand wouldn't shake. *Mental hospital. Tell the*

police I hurt them. E had a knife and was going to cut her arm.
A drop of sweat hit the page, running the ink in the word "knife."
I dropped the pen and sat down on the kitchen floor with my arms
around my knees.

Bethany picked up the note and stared at it for a few moments.
Then she picked up the pen I had dropped. "Stay right here."
She ripped the top page from the pad and began writing. She
never showed me what she wrote, but it took a while for her to
finish. When she was done she set the pad on the kitchen table.
Then she disappeared into her room for what felt like a long time.
The digital clock on the oven said she was only gone for eight
minutes.

"They are not doing this to you," she said when she came back
out. She had a duffel bag and had exchanged her angelic white
robe for her usual all-black street clothes. "I won't let them."
She pulled me up off the floor. I shuffled after her. My head
buzzed like I'd been riding a jackhammer all day.

She opened the door to the garage and stopped so abruptly
I ran into her back. "Ho-lee shit," she said. Seeing why she
stopped, I would have said the same thing had I been able.

9

Bethany didn't say another word until we got out of town and onto Interstate 69. Then she became almost manic. "Dad locks his Beemer in the museum in place of the museum's car whenever he goes to a show. I would have known that if I'd thought about it at all. Nothing to do about it now, I suppose." With her tone of voice, I wouldn't have been at all surprised if she had ended this speech with *dum-dee-dum-dum.*

I was actually glad for the Duesenberg, though; it felt heavy and secure. The engine running at 60 miles per hour in third gear sounded like a World War II bomber—loud, but steady. Unbreakable. I flexed my arms and patted the dash to convey this to Bethany, trying to copy her apparent good mood. She aimed a thumb at the two silver plastic bottles of lead fuel additive in the back seat. "If we want the engine to keep sounding like that we'll need to find as much of that stuff as we can. The cylinders need the extra lubrication the lead gives them." A Honda Civic crawled past in the passing lane, both driver and passenger gaping at us. Bethany waved.

"Could you get the bag from behind my seat?"

I figured she had brought extra clothes, though I had no idea where she was taking me. The bag was too heavy only to be full of clothes.

"I didn't have time to count it," she said. "Just leaf through and see how much we have."

I made such a loud noise when I unzipped the bag that Bethany jumped. She seemed pleased with herself though.

"Dad says that if JP Morgan could keep a million bucks stuffed under his mattress, he doesn't need banks either. Who knows where he heard that, or if it's true, but it rubbed off on me." Her voice became parental. "Now Cliff, I know that looks like a lot of money, but it's my whole savings from the salon. We're on a budget starting right now."

I zipped up the bag again, leaving the money uncounted; suddenly just holding up my head was a real battle. My eyelids kept drooping. Bethany sobered. "Why don't you try to sleep for a while? I won't look for a hotel until we're in Michigan."

Hotel? Michigan? She seemed to have a very detailed plan considering neither of us had known we were going anywhere a few hours ago. But she couldn't read my questions in the dark, and I didn't have the energy to write them anyway. I let my body shut down.

10

Dark, flat land stretches out from the highway in all directions. I am still running; I haven't stopped since my first step out the back door of my house in Auburn. Now, though, instead of running away, I am doing the chasing. The Deusenberg's tail lights burn red pinholes in the darkness ahead. They're not getting any further away, but I am definitely not getting any closer, either.

My mother's voice echoes through the night sky all around me, but it's a small sound, like I'm running inside a tin can and she's yelling into another tin can connected to mine by a string. "Come back, Clifford! Why would you leave me?"

But I don't answer. Of course I don't; I can't answer.

I duck my head and push my legs to move just a little bit faster. It makes no difference. The yellow dashes dividing the highway's two lanes flash by faster and faster until they appear to be one solid streak, like the mark of a yellow highlighter across a particularly interesting—and lengthy—passage in a book. But everything else stays the same. I'm on a treadmill under a spotlight.

Mom's voice is gone. Now there is another sound: a high, somehow massive squeal of metal, like an iron gate swinging open on hinges that haven't seen a drop of oil in decades.

Now I know the real reason I'm running. I don't want to look back but I can't help it. Eleanor is rolling toward me. There's no other way to explain it. She's grasping one foot in each hand, her body contorted into a grotesque sort of wheel, and she's somersaulting after me. Just eating up the highway between us. Each time she rolls I see the black hilt and flashing blade of a J.A. Henckels utility knife in the breast pocket of her jean jacket.

She can see how quickly she's gaining; a high wail of triumph escapes her and fills the night like Mom's voice could not. The second before she overtakes me the wail seems to switch from triumph to dismay. Either way, she rolls over me like wind and the tail lights ahead wink out.

11

"Cliff, it's time to wake up." Mom's voice was soft and gentle. My relief was so great I almost wept. The last days had been a terrible nightmare—Mom was not sick; Eleanor had not threatened to cut herself up and blame it on me; Marguerite certainly was not my new mother. I was back at home and Mom was waking me for breakfast.

It was still dark, though. And I wasn't in bed, I was sitting upright.

"We're at the hotel. I got us a room."

That got my attention. Us? One room? I opened my eyes and saw glowing red 6 set on a blue and white sign.

"It's kind of a crappy place, but who knows how long we'll be on the road? My money won't last forever."

My mind flashed back to my first time sitting in the salon chair, terrified, with Bethany poised over me spraying water into her hand to test its temperature.

She must have been thinking the same thing. "Wow, I haven't seen that expression in a couple years. It's going to be fine. There's a lock on the bathroom door and you can undress in your own bed and everything." She handed me a plastic card and pointed out the windshield. "Room's right there. One-twelve.

I've got my own key. I'm going to get us some food."

My hand froze on the door handle. My dream came screaming back: tail lights in the distance.

"I'm coming back, Cliff. I'm coming back." She laid her hand on my wrist. "I told you I won't leave you. I'm getting something for us to eat. You can even take my duffel bag in. I'll take twenty bucks for the food."

Slowly I nodded. I held up the key card and opened my door. "That boy ain't right," I told her confidently.

"I'll see you in a bit."

I left the duffel bag in the foot well and went to check out our room.

The Waldorf Astoria this was not. The TV was bolted to a metal swing arm, which was bolted to the wall. The remote was velcroed to the side of the TV and further connected by a spiraled black cord. Still, there were no roaches in the bathroom, nor any suspicious hairs in the sheets. And soon Bethany would be here. Right now I couldn't think of a more welcoming place to spend the night.

I stripped down in the roach-free bathroom (the door had a lock, just as Bethany had promised) and turned on the shower. I felt salty after my evening sprint across Auburn, and while I didn't expect any amorous advances from Bethany I figured I might as well be clean when she got back.

The shower was the best surprise the room had to offer. Focused sprays of water beat savagely at my scalp and back in pulsing triple jets. I stood in there for a good fifteen minutes, listening to the water on my skin and trying hard not to think of home, of Marguerite, of Eleanor, of...

Mom.

I had left my dying mother without saying goodbye, I realized. How selfish could I be? I was a terrible and ungrateful son. Tomorrow Mom would wake up and wait for me to show up so we could spend her second day in the hospital together. And all I could do was shower up so I didn't smell like an ox when my girlfriend got back to our hotel room?

My legs felt weak again, as they had earlier at Bethany's house and I crumpled to the floor. That shower stall is where I did most of my mourning for my mother; somehow I knew our life together had come to a close. I didn't cry or beat the wall. I stared at the *gratis* shampoo bottles for awhile; I pulled the waxy paper off the tiny motel soap, but didn't use it; I watched rills of water bead up and eventually run down the inside of the translucent shower curtain. I felt like a marionette whose puppeteer was a five-year-old kid with A.D.D.

There was a timid knock on the bathroom door. "Cliff? Are you about done? I got us Wendy's."

I was freezing. How long had I been sitting here? My hands shook as I turned off the water. "Dude looks like a lady!" I called through chattering teeth, snatching a folded white towel from the rack.

"Okay, your food's on the bed. Hurry before it gets cold."

Despite how cold the shower had gotten, the mirror was still fogged up and a heavy mist made the tile floor slick. Drying off warmed me up.

Bethany was sitting cross-legged on her bed with wrappers strewn around her on the comforter. *The Blues Brothers* was on TV. "I tried to wait for you, but I got hungry," she said. "There's ketchup packets in the bag there. And I got you a Frosty."

She looked so beautiful, with her square black glasses, black lipstick (she had abandoned her lip rings about a year ago), and wonderful black hair, I wanted to throw my arms around her and tell her thank you until my voice went hoarse. Instead I secured my towel around my waist and sat down for supper.

12

I woke up before Bethany. A plastic blue Wal Mart bag was on the floor beside her bed, and I poked through it as quietly as I could. There were a couple shirts in there, including a nice button-down dress shirt, a pair of khaki cargo pants, some socks, several pairs of distinctly male underpants, and various toiletries. Best of all, a stack of legal pads and a package of pens.

My poking wasn't quiet enough. "I would have shown them to you last night, but you were too cute in your little towel," Bethany said, sitting up in her bed. I was still in my towel—I had slept in it—and suddenly very conscious of the fact. Bethany must have noticed because she turned away. "Go ahead," she said to the opposite wall. "Try that stuff on. I won't look."

I dropped my towel awkwardly and yanked up the first pair of underpants I grabbed. "Wear the nice shirt," she said, still facing away. "Are you dressed?"

"He slimed me," I said.

She rolled back over. "Ooh la la, very handsome." She appraised me for a moment longer. "I have to get ready too." She stood up on the bed and let the blankets fall around her feet. She was wearing a long T-shirt and, for all I could tell, nothing else. "I'm going to shower, then we'll need to leave." She stretched her arms up and wiggled her fingers luxuriantly. She *was* wearing something else, I saw: shiny high-cut underpants. Black, naturally. The muscles in her legs twitched.

I looked away before my eyes could fall out. I heard her hop off the bed and pad into the bathroom. I heard the door swing shut, but didn't hear it latch. Surely she wouldn't…

She did. A sliver of light shone invitingly between the door and the jamb. That was the last straw. I ripped the plastic from the legal pads and took a brand new pen from the package. I must have written and rewritten that note ten times while she hummed in the shower:

Bethany, I don't understand…
Bethany, what's happening with…
Bethany, why are you…
Bethany, do you want…

Each sentence felt like more of an accusation than the last. She came out of the bathroom to find me hunched over the legal pad with several balled-up pages on the bed and floor around me. Bars of sunlight fell through the curtains across my bed as if into a jail cell. She had one of the white towels wrapped around her middle and one piled on top of her head. "Cliff, what's wrong?"

The pen lay uselessly on the pad. This time I had begun with, *Bethany, you are beautiful like no other woman has been beautiful to me. I'm just confused about*

She understood right away. Her hands gently pulled my head to her bare shoulder. "Don't be sorry. I should be the one…

"Listen to me." Now her hands turned my face toward hers. Without thick glasses to hide them, her eyes were clear and wonderful. "I am doing the only thing I can think of to help you. And I want to do it as much as I want to help you." She let go and I sank back onto her shoulder. "I'm sorry you're confused. And don't you dare apologize again. There's nothing for you to be sorry for."

She smelled like the lilacs in Mom's old garden and hotel soap. I put my arms around her and breathed her scent until she said, "I need to get dressed so we can go."

The Henry L. Brown Municipal Building in Coldwater, Michigan is a white fortress of glass and concrete. Sunlight glinted off the glass dome rising above the main entrance. Bethany parked the Duesenberg in the back parking lot; we were still close enough to home that someone might recognize the car from the museum and start asking awkward questions.

Inside, a pretty, middle-aged receptionist sat behind a circular wooden desk in the center of a large rotunda. Without preamble Bethany said, "Where do we go for a civil union?"

It took a couple seconds for her words to sink in. Then my whole body spasmed and went numb like I had just stuck all my fingers and toes into one big electric socket. The receptionist glanced at me from the corner of her eye as she answered Bethany. "Have you completed the application?" She was really staring now. "Is he alright?" she finally asked.

"He's fine," Bethany said. "We're just really excited."

"Do you need to vomit, young man? There's a restr—"

"Where do we get an application?"

I almost couldn't hear her over the roar of blood in my ears. My face must have been purple.

The receptionist pointed at an archway behind her. "Up those stairs, first door on your right."

Bethany thanked her and pulled me away from the desk.

"Congratulations," the receptionist called after us.

The next hour was a haze. Bethany shoved papers in front of me and pointed where I was supposed to sign, which I did. As we were leaving, I heard a secretary tell Bethany the application would take twenty-four hours to process, and we could come back tomorrow morning for the ceremony.

"I should have told you," Bethany said once we were back in the car.

My eyes bugged and I nodded like a bobble-head doll.

"But I was afraid you might not come if I did. You weren't thinking clearly."

ME? I wanted to shout.

"Cliff, the only way to keep Marguerite from being your new mother is for you to be independent. Emancipated." She started the car. "In Michigan you can get married without a parent's consent when you're seventeen," she said. "One of my friends did it in high school. Pissed her mom off something fierce."

Independent. Married and independent. I took her hand in both of mine and stared at her. Her eyes flitted to the dashboard and around the interior, as if seeking an escape hatch. Finally she looked at me and smiled, but she pulled her hand from mine. "Let's just get this done with. We can figure out the rest for as long as it takes."

On the way back to the hotel room, Bethany told me she was going to call her dad. She offered to call Mom too, even though I could tell she was not looking forward to it. I doubted hearing Bethany's voice say we were getting married would help Mom in any way, and it might incite Marguerite to do something desperate to reclaim me. After reading my note Bethany agreed and squeezed my leg between shifting gears and fooling with the spark knob on the steering wheel.

When we got back I went straight into the bathroom, locked the door, and turned on the overhead fan; future wife or not, I decided Bethany should have the chance to explain everything to her dad in private. Mostly though I just stared into my own eyes in the mirror and let my brain pace in its cage.

I'm going to marry Bethany.

Bethany's going to marry me.

Mom's dying.

Eleanor was really going to cut herself, wasn't she?

"...packaged up in a nice white jacket..."

I'm getting married.

I didn't say goodbye.

"Cliff!" Bethany pounded on the bathroom door. "CLIFF!" She sounded terrified.

I almost wrenched the door off its hinges. Before it swung completely open Bethany barreled through and wrapped her arms around me. I held her fiercely, waiting for the worst: her dad had the cops after us, maybe; or he'd disowned her for stealing his most prized possession. I was prepared for anything except for what she told me.

"Cliff, I'm so sorry. I'm so sorry."

What was *she* sorry about? She was the one who had saved me from...

I untangled her and held her at arm's length. One look at her eyes and I knew.

"I never should have taken you away, Cliff. I'm so sorry."

All I could do was shake my head. I wanted to tell her that she didn't need to be sorry—that I was the one who ran away. I also wanted to tell her not say what she'd heard from her dad. As long as she didn't say it I could go on hoping I was wrong.

But instead of telling her all that I just went on shaking my head.

So she said it: "Your mom died this morning around three."

When I hit the floor my teeth clicked together hard enough that I saw stars.

"Marguerite called my dad this morning—got him out of bed—to see if you were there."

I had been wrong about Bethany being terrified; she was furious. "Dad told me to call the police and turn you in. Marguerite told him...Shit, what a..." she searched for a noun foul enough to call Aunt Marguerite and came up empty. She continued, "She told him you'd gone crazy, just like you said she would, and that you'd attacked her and Eleanor."

Bits of black and green danced around in my vision.

"Eleanor's in the hospital with a broken arm. Marguerite said you threw kitchen appliances at them and they had to hide until you took off. Funny *she's* not hurt," Bethany spat, "just Eleanor.

"Dad said he understands I care about you, but you're not stable, and what if you hurt me because you're so upset?" She sat down beside me and held my head to her chest. "He didn't even mention the car."

We sat in silence, Bethany clutching my head and rocking back and forth on the cold tile. I felt like I'd gone about fifteen rounds with Oscar de la Hoya.

"I told Dad we're in Chicago," Bethany said slowly. "When Marguerite calls Dad again, he'll point west." She kissed my forehead. "Still, we can't stay here; it doesn't matter that you're emancipated if she calls the cops and tells them you tried to kill your own aunt and cousin." She sighed again. "Tomorrow afternoon we'll have to move again. Any direction but west, I suppose."

My head cleared instantly. Finally I could steer this rollercoaster my life had become. Marguerite's shining eyes and Eleanor's deathly grin came floating back from Christmas ten years ago.

Freaks go there, Marguerite had said about Prince Edward Island.

Yes. That is where we would go. If I were in a different country Marguerite wouldn't keep looking for me; she just wanted me out of her life.

I turned up to Bethany and kissed her soundly on the mouth. She seemed surprised, but took it in stride, and even lingered a moment.

"What was that for?"

I stood and marched out of the bathroom for a pad and pen to share my plan with Bethany.

13

At ten o'clock the next morning a secretary at the municipal building steered us into the small courtroom where the judge would perform the service. Judge Cairo was a short man with a heavy beard and black horn rims to rival Bethany's. He managed to look kind despite his owlish appearance. "It does my heart good to see young people in love," he said from behind the bench. We stood before him awkwardly—I doubted we looked like we were in love.

"This is not a complicated procedure," he said. "Clifford Carlson and Bethany Wray, you have filed for a civil union."

Bethany and I glanced at one another.

"Thereby you will enjoy the legal rights and privileges granted to a married couple. Do you understand?"

My ears rang in the silence. Dust motes big enough to eat hung in the sun beams falling through the windows. Bethany and I exchanged glances again and then nodded.

"Good. For the record, are you each willing participants in this union?"

Here it was. The big "I do." This was not at all as I had imagined my wedding day. Bethany was beautiful, though, inside and out. I had daydreamed about us getting married since the first time she cut my hair. I loved her spiky hair, all the zippers in her jacket and skirt. I loved that she made me feel interesting and likeable.

Her cold fingers linked with mine. She rubbed the back of my thumb with her own. "I am willing," she said.

The judge bobbed his head, more like an owl than ever, and turned to me. I suddenly had to answer. I had to do this for Bethany, who had stolen a bazillion-dollar car and left her home for me, who was *marrying* me to keep me from getting locked in a mental institution.

She was reaching in her purse to get some paper. "Do you have a pen, Cliff?" she whispered.

I squeezed her hand and shook my head. I would answer the judge or die trying. *I am willing*, my brain sent to my vocal cords and mouth. Eleanor had taught me to say that ridiculous string of syllables as a name, I could do this!

I am willing.

Sweat dripped into my eyes.

I am willing.

My tongue felt like a hot loaf of bread in my mouth. I couldn't breathe.

I AM WILLING.

"I love Yoo-Hoo!" I gasped.

My eyes stayed shut and my tongue shrank back to its normal size. I stood that way, listening to the dizzy rush of my own breathing until Bethany squeezed my hand again. When I opened my eyes, the judge was leaned back in his seat, a mixture of curiosity and horror on his round face.

"Just write it down, it's okay," Bethany whispered. Her voice sounded odd. "Nerves," she told the judge.

My penmanship was clear at least. The judge accepted my note. "I'll sign as witness since you brought none of your own. There. By the power granted to me by the state of Michigan, I pronounce you legally married." His jowls drew up as he smiled at us. "Until death do you part and so forth. Congratulations. I'll pass the appropriate papers to my secretary outside. After she notarizes your license you can be on your way."

"Thank you, sir."

I wondered if we should stay standing in front of the bench until the judge left, but he just stayed in his seat and Bethany took my hand and pulled me from the room.

Stepping out of the municipal building, I breathed in the sunshine and scent of mown grass thinking I'd never known anything finer. Bethany whooped and threw her arms around my neck. "My husband!" she hollered, and kissed me. "Let's celebrate."

We had checked out of the motel before our appointment with the judge. Bethany had agreed quickly and enthusiastically to my proposed final destination. I built a sturdy, menacing iron door in my mind, like Tolkien's Black Gate of Mordor, to keep out stray guilty thoughts of Mom, my fears of Marguerite—anything that would make today unpleasant. Bethany seemed to have done something similar. It was working for both of us so far.

"Screw Wendy's," she said, her arms still slung around my neck. "We're going someplace nice. Denny's nice." She struggled to keep a straight face.

I leaned over to give her a piggyback ride. "If I walk, the movie will be over," I said.

Her smile faded. "Cliff, your back isn't—" she began.

I patted my shoulder. "I barfed on an anthill."

The smile came back. "Okay, hold still." She put her hands on my shoulders and heaved herself onto my back, hissing through her teeth like Mom used to when she thought something might hurt me. "How's that?"

I held her hamstrings and bounced her a few times to get her legs settled on my hips. I'd never given anyone a piggyback ride. It was fun—my shoulder didn't hurt at all.

"Don't hurry," she whispered into my ear, and began kissing my neck.

If I hadn't been so conscious of people staring at us, I would have taken the rest of my life getting back to the car.

14

The first leg of our trip made both of us uneasy. We bought an Atlas at the Wal Mart in Coldwater, along with some bread and deli turkey for supper. The problem was that we had to drive south on I-69 back into the northeastern tip of Indiana, only about twenty minutes from home. The landscape was familiar, but now unwelcoming. Every highway patrol or state trooper made my stomach leap into my throat. From the way her hands gripped the wheel like she was crushing a deadly snake whenever a cruiser passed on the other side of the median, Bethany felt it too.

Very quickly, though, we hit the Indiana-soon-to-be-Ohio Turnpike, and within an hour Bethany was humming to herself and tapping rhythmless beats on the wheel. Near Elyria we left the turnpike for I-90, north all the way to Buffalo, New York, where we stopped for the night. Bethany's duffel bag had a slow bleed from the gas-chugging Duesenberg, so we decided to stick with our thrifty motel of choice from Coldwater.

She took care of the reservation again. When she got back she was disappointed the clerk hadn't asked for any proof of marriage when she asked for a single room with two occupants.

The legal papers were burning a hole in her pocket, she said. "I want someone besides Judge Barn Owl to be happy for us."

I was certainly happy for us, if anxious to the point of nausea. Kissing her in the bathroom last night was all fine and good, but we'd had separate sleeping arrangements afterward.

Bethany didn't speak as she pulled the Duesenberg up to our room door. She was good; when I still had the beige Corolla, sometimes I had to back out and pull into a space two or three times before I was in the middle. The Duesenberg, from what I could tell, handled like an aircraft carrier, but she always made berth right between the lines on the first try.

"I'll get the food out of the back," she said. "You want to bring in the duffel bag?"

I nodded. The duffel bag, in addition to our money, had all our clothes—the ones she packed and the ones she'd bought me two days ago. Some devious portion of my mind dedicated to being almost eighteen wondered if she would want me to model any of my new underpants. I was immediately glad it was dark out and Bethany couldn't see me blushing.

The room was about like the other one: clean sheets, locking bathroom, sequestered TV.   Bethany seemed at home, lying on the bedspread channel surfing. But I kept staring at the bed. I must have stood in the doorway for a full minute when she finally grumped at me to close the door, did I want to let in all the bugs in New York?

She excused herself to the shower. "I feel so gamey being in a car all day. *Blues Brothers* is on HBO again," she said dryly. "You can catch the parts you missed the other night."

To my great relief—and simultaneous disappointment—she actually closed and locked the bathroom door for her shower. When she emerged fifteen minutes later she again had a single towel covering her torso, but nothing else. Her hair, black and clean and perfect, hung in a tidy arc meeting on either side of her chin, minus the spikes.

"Your turn," she said, pointing a thumb at the bathroom.

I nodded and stood. At this point, if she'd told me to wash my hair in the toilet I would have. Just as I was swinging the door shut, a damp towel landed on my head. Before I even thought about it I turned around to give Bethany my best irritated *What was that for?* expression, but in mid-turn the appropriate neurons fired and I realized where the towel had come from. Bethany sat innocently against the headboard, covered by the bedspread. "There was only one towel," she said. "I was just giving it to you." She grinned wickedly. "If you'd rather come back out here for it after your shower—"

I dove into the bathroom and slammed the door.

15

Bethany and I only had one night to enjoy being married. The good news is that, had we known it would be our last night together, I don't think either of us would have changed anything. No regret but that time had to move forward.

And we moved with it: I-90 took us all the way across New York, dipping south at Albany to cut a bowl shape through Massachusetts up to Exeter, Vermont, where it became I-95. I had planned our route yesterday in the car, and we arrived in Bangor, Maine about half an hour after the sun had set at our backs.

Bethany said we needed fuel for the third time in less than 700 miles. "If we gas up tonight, we can leave in the morning with one less thing to worry about." She pulled up to the pump nearest to the convenience store and reached in the back for a silver bottle of lead additive. "You want to pull a couple bucks from the bag and get us some drinks for the room tonight?" Her eyes flashed. "If last night was any indication, we'll need them."

I thought in a year or two I might stop blushing, but for now, every time I thought about the night before—or the nights to come, for that matter—blood rushed up to my head like mercury climbing a thermometer on the sun. Bethany's joke for the day was to ask over and over if we should pick up some aloe in the next town for my sunburn.

I leaned over and kissed her before getting out of the car. *Preview of coming attractions*, I wrote, blushing furiously again.

Bethany giggled and stepped out of the car.

Almost unconsciously I headed straight for the Dr. Pepper and pulled out a six-pack. I hadn't even known until the day before that it was Bethany's favorite.

"That your car?" The cashier, who had a white handlebar mustache wider than his own face, had been staring at the Duesenberg since I walked in.

I nodded.

"Mighty fine," he said. "I'd be careful o' them boys outside, though. They might just be admirin', but they might not, too, if you ken."

My head whipped up from counting the bills in my hand. Three young men, two of whom could have been the skinny younger brothers of Eminem, had effectively surrounded the car: one standing at the grill and one each at the driver and passenger door. Bethany had gotten back into the car, but I saw the fuel pump still stuck in the tank. The tallest one, by Bethany's door, was talking, but I couldn't hear what he was saying.

I slammed the money down on the counter beside the Dr. Pepper and barreled through the glass doors without either. "Hey you!" I called. "Get your damn hands off her!" My voice even had Crispin Glover's lisp.

Bethany, still inside the car, met my gaze for a split second. The terror I saw in her eyes was for me, not herself. In that one moment, for the first time, I knew she loved me. Sure, she'd taken terrible risks on my behalf—not to mention marrying me—but now I knew why. I wasn't just charity to her; I was her husband.

"The fuck do you care, Rambo?" the tallest one said. Eminems 1 and 2 snickered. "This your ride?" He jerked his head at Bethany, still inside. "Is the car yours too?"

The Eminem 1, at the grill, leaned over and pounded the Duesenberg's hood in glee. "You crack my shit up, Terry."

I couldn't answer out loud, but "Terry" must have seen me tighten when he pointed at Bethany. "Yeah," he grinned. "You and the Queen of the Damned. Look, man, I was just enjoying your fine, ah, wheels here. Nothing to get wrapped up about." He backed away from the car, his hands out at his sides, palms up. "It's a really fine piece."

Eminem 1 cackled again, but at least he and his clone were following Terry away. Eventually they stepped out of the island of light around the gas pumps and their voices died away.

My heart was pounding, and I berated myself for it. They guy was a jackass certainly, but he wasn't dangerous. Of course the Duesenberg was going to draw attention from all sorts of people. I sure hadn't seen one on the road before.

Dr. Pepper. I'd forgotten it inside. The old attendant had made my change and bagged it up with my drinks. "Punks is what they are," he said. "Crawl out like locusts on these warm nights."

Outside I saw Bethany quickly hang up the nozzle and get back into the car. I set a twenty and a five on the counter for the gas.

"'s on me," he said, waving his yellowed fingers at me. "Just seeing such a fine car is payment enough for me."

I nodded my thanks and took the bag.

"Fine car and a fine night for drivin' it."

For the third time in as many minutes, I nodded to him, hoping it would serve as both agreement and farewell.

The glass door had barely swung shut when they struck. They came from the left, around the side of the gas station. Terry's shoulder slammed into my upper arm. He must have been running pretty fast when he hit me because I skidded several feet, discarding much of the skin from my forehead and cheek on the concrete. The rest of it, as they say, was a blur. I remember lying on my side, hugging my knees; fists, sneakers, and saliva striking me wherever they could reach. I don't remember any sound besides a deep tympanic vibration whenever a blow struck its target, and the scuffing of their shoe soles on the concrete.

I only heard their voices at the end: a grunt from Terry and high shouts from the Eminems. Hot, stinking breath blew into my face, and it was a moment before I figured out it must be exhaust fumes from a car. A harsh ringing built steadily louder, like a chorus of wet fingers tracing the rims of crystal wine goblets, until I thought my head would burst with it. Darkness beckoned me away from that sound, from car exhaust, from Terry and his biting hands and feet. I followed.

16

"Get the hell out of here!"

I thought I must be dreaming again. I opened my eyes and caught a glimpse of Bethany, standing beside my bed in a hospital room, red faced, before I had to squeeze them shut against a powerful wave of nausea. There had also been a blur of pink and stonewashed blue at the corner of my vision. The blue, at least, was very familiar.

The dark behind my eyelids kept spinning, but it was better than the light outside them. I decided just to listen.

"Now, now, Elvira," said Eleanor's voice. "You're in enough trouble for kidnapping my dear helpless cousin."

"Helpless?" Bethany's voice was dripping with menace. "Gosh, Eleanor, I thought he attacked you and your mom at the same time. Can I see the scars, by the way? I hear you nearly cut off your own arm. Is that why you have the cast? Did the doctors have to reattach your arm?"

Eleanor was silent.

"And as for the trouble I'm in: kidnappers don't often marry their victims, do they?"

Eleanor honked. She must have meant it to be a sound of contempt, but it sounded more like a sob. "The day anyone marries Helen Keller here—"

I heard papers rustling—Bethany finally got to show off our marriage license.

"Let me see that," Eleanor said. Even with my eyes closed I could imagine how she was standing: her huge head tipped impossibly to one side on her beanstalk neck, one bony hand on her equally bony hips (the denim jacket supposedly hiding her bony elbows), the other stretched out in certainty that Bethany would obey.

Not that she would. Bethany was smart enough not to give anything important to my cousin, especially if it helped me out...

More rustling, as the papers changed hands. *Bethany, what are you doing?* I tried to shout. I must have made some sound. "Did he say something?" Bethany said. "Cliff, are you awake?"

I braced myself for the nausea and opened my eyes to see my wife's wonderful, hopeful face hovering over my own. "Hi, Hon—"

Her eyes widened and went out of focus at the dry, purposeful sound of Eleanor shredding our marriage license.

"We're not *from* Michigan," Eleanor said, as if she were telling a child the earth was not flat. Bethany was frozen in time. "*My* papers are from Indiana, and they say Clifford is dangerous, and must be admitted to the nearest appropriate institution for the safety of himself and his family. He's already attacked us once, no matter what you believe, Elvira. Plus he's a minor for another week. As his legal guardian, my mom would never allow him to marry you anyway."

"Seventeen-year-olds don't need permission to get married in Michigan, you dumb cunt," Bethany said softly. I'd never heard her use that word before. She sounded more resigned than angry, which somehow made the vulgarity even more disturbing. She turned and stalked toward Eleanor.

Eleanor, finally showing some sense, appeared terrified. I saw that the pink blur from before was a fiberglass cast wrapped around her left arm, which she now held out sideways in front of her as if baiting an attack dog. "Don't you come near me. I can have you put away too."

But Bethany just kept moving right out the door, as if in a trance, and with her my hopes that this night could still turn out well. Bethany, who said she would never leave me—my *wife*, for heaven's sake—was gone.

Eleanor stood still for a moment, staring at the door, apparently in as much disbelief as I was. Then she turned to me. "You guys are married?"

I didn't even look at her.

"Why'd you take that stupid car, anyway?" Eleanor suddenly yelled. "You might as well have left a trail of gold pieces behind you. It looks like John D. Rockefeller's hearse. Nobody misses that thing when it goes by." She was all eyes and mouth. "Mom is buying me a makeover, like on those TV shows. She's going to make me beautiful." She was actually crying. "You didn't have to make it so easy to find you, Clifford. You didn't." She sounded like she was five years old, scolding a stuffed animal for ruining imaginary tea time. "All I had to do was try."

She sat on the edge of my bed. "I guess I finally did something right."

Part 3:
Bethany

1

Listening to that idiot scarecrow yap about legal papers and her responsibility to keep Cliff safe was as pointless as it was enraging. A phone call in the morning would get a new wedding license in the mail, and I could ask the nurse to get Cliff some food, now that he was awake.

When I stepped out the door there were two police officers at the nurse's station outside Cliff's room. The nearest one tapped the other on the arm and walked up to me. "Are you Bethany Carlson?"

I had never heard my married name out loud before. I decided it sounded pretty good. "Yes."

"Will you come outside with us please?"

Two more officers in the parking lot hunkered down by the Model J. They reminded me of casual visitors at Dad's museum.

When they saw me approaching, however, they were anything but casual. The taller one, whom my mind inexplicably dubbed Hightower, pulled a pad and pen from his pocket. The gesture reminded me so much of Cliff, a lump rose in my throat. "Mrs. Carlson? Can you please tell us what happened at the Gas 'n' Go?"

Relating the story was more than surreal standing in the parking lot with the red and blue lights flashing in their harsh orbits, momentarily highlighting surrounding cars, trees, and houses. Halfway through I began shivering and Hightower offered to take my statement from inside the cruiser, but I shook my head and carried on:

"The Mark Twain guy who worked the counter came shuffling out the door rubbing his eyes like he'd just woken up and staring at the jerk who attacked Cliff.

"I couldn't help staring either; his legs were bent in all the wrong places. Wet black spots were blossoming in different parts of his jeans. He tried to sit up but couldn't, and he kept saying, 'What the…? What the…? What the…?'

"Cliff was in little better shape. I felt him breathing when I pulled his head away from the exhaust pipe, so I knew he was alive."

Here I had another brief shivering fit, remembering how close I had come to running over Cliff when I rammed the ringleader.

"He didn't respond when I said his name. And his eyes were rolled back in his head.

I had a hard time containing my fury with the station attendant all over again when I described asking him repeatedly where the nearest hospital was. He had just stared at the guy I'd hit, rubbing a shaky hand over his whiskers and licking his index finger like he had a book somewhere that needed its pages turned. When he did speak, he asked me if I would take the injured guy to the hospital too.

"He probably would have fit in the back seat," I told Mahoney (I had confessed too much to start being dishonest now), "but I was too angry to help him. So I told the attendant to call 911 and explain what happened. He gave me a city map and told me to come here. I gave him my name and license plate number so you could find me if you needed."

The officers glanced at each other. Hightower stopped taking notes put away his paper. The short one (as long as I was handing out names, this one might as well be Mahoney; he resembled Steve Gutenberg as much as his partner did Bubba Smith) gave an almost imperceptible nod and the two who had met me upstairs retreated to their cruisers. "I appreciate your cooperation so far. Believe me, giving your name and plates to the attendant was a smart move. It's the main reason you aren't in cuffs right now." He glanced at the Hightower again. "We just need you to come to the station yet to identify—"

I started shaking my head. Cliff was half-wrecked and stuck with that horrible banshee cousin of his.

"Please, ma'am," Mahoney said. "You've been helpful so far. We'll have you back here in a few hours."

"If you knew I was here you must have the injured guy in custody already. He wasn't running anywhere. And I doubt his buddies would or could carry him. They might have had a hundred-fifty pounds between them."

"Those 'buddies' are who we need your help with. We're pretty sure we've got the right guys; the Gas 'n' Go attendant said there were two of them besides the leader, but, like you said yourself, he wasn't seeing clearly, and he could not make a positive ID."

Hightower saw my internal wavering. "This is the only way you can be sure the people responsible for putting your husband in the hospital receive proper justice. It won't take long."

They were being nice; I guessed that if I refused they could subpoena me, or whatever it might be called, stuff me in the back of their car, and force me to perform my civic duty. I owed it to Cliff to send these guys up the river if I could.

I nodded. Mahoney sighed loudly, relieved, I suppose, that I hadn't made things even more difficult. Hightower opened the rear door of his car like a chauffeur and I got in.

2

The lineup was a cakewalk. Both boys who helped beat up Cliff stood against the measuring wall, shifting their weight and nervously glancing at each other. Twice Mahoney got on the intercom and told them to stand still. The only other person who looked anything like them (short, sharp features, bleached hair) had arms like tree trunks and was thus ruled out.

Mahoney smirked slightly when he informed the men in the lineup they could turn to their right and exit. I actually felt sorry for the boys for a moment; without the influence of their now-broken leader they would probably be parked in front of a Nintendo right now, punching each other's scrawny arms and giggling, drinking bottles of Mountain Dew, bopping to rap music, and hurting no one at all.

Then I remembered their tendon-popping grins while they'd kicked Cliff—curled up and offering no defense—simply because he'd quoted the wrong movie to their boss.

I was glad I'd come.

3

Hightower dropped me off at the Model J around midnight, a mere two hours after we'd left—Mahoney had stayed behind to finish the paperwork, he said. I thanked him for keeping his promise of brevity at the station.

I unlocked the car to get some money from my bag. I wanted to buy some actual food from the cafeteria before I went to Cliff's room; a bag of chips from a vending machine didn't seem celebratory enough for the occasion. Lunch had been at a Taco Bell in Vermont, and felt like three days ago.

I bought a Caesar Salad in a clear plastic box and jogged up the stairs to Cliff's room. It was empty. The sheets on his bed were a clean white and folded so precisely they appeared starched. Maybe they'd already discharged Cliff and parked him in a waiting room for me to pick him up and go home. I knew hospitals didn't like keeping patients very long if they didn't have to.

The attendant who'd admitted Cliff was gone for the evening. A pretty, young girl sat at the nurse's station in a green smock. "Hi," I said to her.

"Hi." She beamed. Way too chipper for the graveyard shift.

"My husband was in room three-twenty earlier this evening.

Not even two hours ago."

The prom queen leafed through a pile of manila folders on the desk. "Three-twenty...Carlson?"

"That's right." I suddenly had a whopper of a headache—a migraine that grabbed my eyeballs from behind and squeezed in time with my heartbeat.

She affected an expression of deep concern, drawing in her glossy lips and penciled brows. It was very cute.

My eyeballs throbbed.

"They said you would call," she said, opening the file she'd extracted. "There were no problems. Patient Carlson, Clifford has already been transferred."

Transferred. Not discharged. What injuries could they not handle at this hospital? Dark, ugly names for what might be wrong with Cliff flashed through my mind: *internal hemorrhaging; kidney failure; brain aneurism; ruptured spleen.* Where else had those bastards hit him? Could the real problem be even worse?

The girl was still talking.

"I'm sorry, what?"

"He was deemed in safe condition for transport to the Bangor Mental Health Institute."

"Where? Who said...? Where?" I thought of the guy I'd run over, and how shock had turned him into a parrot: *What the...? What the...? What the...?*

"Oh, don't worry, Mrs. Carlson. BMHI is the best hospital in Maine."

"Who moved him?" I finally got out.

She frowned. "But..." She was adorable when she was confused. "I thought you were Mrs. Carlson. Your name is on the—" The girl's mouth made a dainty O; a light bulb must have popped on in her head and the sensation surprised her. She spoke officially: "I'm afraid I will have to see your identification if you want me to answer any more questions."

I couldn't help laughing. Braying, even, right in her face. I was too tired and too bitter to do anything else. Eleanor had apparently forged my name to get him out of the hospital and this little toy wanted to see *my* identification? "The damage is done, sweetie," I told her.

4

The nurse at BMHI's welcome desk wasn't nearly as cute as the one at the hospital had been. She looked like she was wearing a wine barrel under her smock. Her thick upper arms jutted from her sleeves like bowling pins. But whatever she lacked in appearance she made up for in terseness. "Name?"

"Bethany Wray," I said. "Carlson, I mean—Cliff's my husband." The nurse squinted at me. How long had it been since I'd slept? "I am Bethany Carlson," I enunciated. I was distantly aware of the clack of keys on her keyboard. "My husband Cliff is a patient here. He transferred a few hours ago from—"

"No patients with the name Carlson."

I rocked back on my heels as if she'd punched me in the face. Eleanor had convinced this gladiator of a nurse to lie for her? The message finally hit home: Marguerite had won. Cliff was gone. I had to grab the edge of the desk to keep my balance.

No. Not yet. I still had leverage. "Excuse me, but I am the patient's wife."

The nurse cocked an eyebrow. "If we had such a patient, and if he was your spouse, you obviously would know he could receive no visitors until at least twenty-four hours after being admitted." She sat back smugly. "I suggest you come back tomorrow morning and bring legal proof of—"

I lost control. "How *dare* you. Cliff is my husband, for God's sake! Why the fuck would I be running around in the middle of the fucking night asking to see some random lunatic I don't even know? What FUN!" I screamed.

The nurse rose out of her seat, her smug expression long gone. "Ma'am, if you don't calm down I'll have to call security."

I ignored her. My wrath was all for Marguerite. She had put Cliff in here. And she'd only gotten away with it because she'd wrecked his brain as a baby and now he couldn't talk to defend himself. And for what? Because he had been a cuter baby than hers? "THAT STUPID WHORE BITCH!" My tenuous grip on the nurse's desk failed and I collapsed on the hard tile floor. Soft beeps from behind the desk told me the nurse was calling security. "Why can't she leave us alone?"

Some force pulled me up by my armpits and set me on unsteady feet. My boots looked blurry and heavy, like they were at the bottom of a swimming pool. I lacked the strength to move them.

"Miss, you are leaving the building," a stern male voice said. "If you do not cooperate we will have to press charges."

I let the rough hands carry me. Right now they were stronger than I could ever be on my own.

The warm night air felt good on my wet face and in my lungs. I managed to get inside my car, crawl into the back seat, and lock the doors before I passed out.

The temperature inside the car was probably in the nineties when I woke up. The seat was slicked with sweat wherever my skin had touched it while I slept. A runner of saliva connected the corner of my mouth to a smaller puddle under my head. I had an incredible headache from crying so hard last night, but my thoughts were clear. Even my anger with Eleanor had waned; she was only Marguerite's puppet. If I wanted shut of that branch of Carlsons—and boy did I—I would have to settle up with the matriarch. That meant going back to Indiana.

♪

"Daddy?"

"Bethany? Oh, thank you God. I thought you weren't going to call again. Where are you?"

I figured my well of tears would be dry after last night, but hearing my dad's voice, so scared and so relieved at the same time, I found myself spilling the events of the last five days in short, broken sentences between sobs. "I'm in Maine—They won't let me see Cliff—Eleanor took—I mean Marguerite—I'm so sorry I took the car—"

And on and on. The only part I left out was getting married; that seemed like something I should share in person. Dad obviously wasn't following what I said anyway, because after his first question: "Maine?" he just emitted random comforts into the phone until I ran out of breath.

"Bethany," he said after I had finished. "Do you have your Triple A card?"

"Yuh-yes," I managed.

"Call the number, tell them you need a flatbed wrecker to bring you back to Auburn."

"Daddy, I'm—" I sniffed wetly. "I'm fine to drive."

"I think we've put enough miles on the Model J for this year," he said dryly. "Go have some lunch, calm down, and call Triple A." I could tell he was relieved the emotional storm had passed. "Make sure they bring a flatbed," he repeated.

"I know. I'll see you in a couple days. Thank you."

"I love you. Come straight home."

6

Glittering blue smoke slinks down the path from the cave toward me like satiny lingerie cascading to a woman's ankles. My breath roars like a waterfall inside my steel helmet, drowning all other sound, but I imagine I hear the echo of another great bellows, this one deep inside the mountain. In my mind's eye I see a gout of dancing blue sparks each time the dragon exhales, briefly illuminating her bony snout and the sharp ridge above one of her horrible eyes, open just enough to let out a ribbon of cold golden light.

A loud crack cuts through my nightmarish daydream and I look down through the slots in my faceplate.

A bone lay broken under my steel boot. A long, dusty, cartoonish femur, with a heavy worn ball for the hip joint and four white knobs at the knee end. The clarity of this bone against the dull ash blanketing the path and rocks all around the cave convinces me this isn't a dream.

This is what you wanted, *a voice in my head reminds me.* You decided to do this all by yourself, and now that you're here it's fight or flight. But if you fly, you can never come back again, she'll make sure of that once she sees you're strong enough to try once.

I yank off my helmet and toss it aside, unable to listen to my own terrified breathing any longer. It kicks up a cloud of silver ash and rolls into the bushes which somehow manage to live here even though the sun must never be visible through the clouds pouring from that cave.

The bushes convince me all over again that this is no dream. In a dream there would only be stone.

Now that my helmet is gone, there is no sound. No wind moaning through cracks in the mountain, or rustling the horribly real bushes lining my path.

Wait.

There is *a sound.*

I had expected the cracking bone to wake the dragon and bring her barreling up the cave from her nest, scaly legs pistoning into the cave floor with deep bass booms that would send birds into panicked flight for miles around.

However, this is not what I hear. Instead there is a soft leathery rhythm, much like the breathing I had imagined earlier. The pounding of dragon feet would have been horrible enough, but this near-silence is much worse.

She's flying, *I realize.* She's flying up to meet me so I won't hear her coming.

She doesn't appear gradually; one moment she is deep in her cave, the next she is high above me, flapping those nearly silent wings and stirring up ash and bone dust. And she is beautiful: gleaming red scales, seemingly of polished metal; the same sensuous blue smoke all around us eking from her nostrils and the corners of her long mouth like the intoxicating smoke from the Caterpillar's hookah *in* Through the Looking Glass. *Her body curves gracefully as she hovers over me, contemplating me from behind the frozen gold glow of her eyes.*

Before either of us can act, all of the bushes on either side of the path begin rustling. Clean white hands, startling in the gloom, shoot from the bush nearest me and scrabble against my gauntlet for purchase.

7

Towns like Auburn can go for years without changing. I had only been gone for just over a week, but I had changed so much in those days, I expected the town to be totally different too. The McDonalds on Main Street was typically empty (townspeople scorned national chains in support of local restaurateurs); the tow-truck's wheels growled on Pike, the old rumbling cobblestone street that Dad said had lulled me to sleep without fail when I was a baby; the rusted train tracks by the museum still needed a visit from an industrial grade weed whacker. I was home.

With one exception: I had never seen police cars at the museum before. Now there were two of them parked in front of the museum—fully one half of Auburn's automotive police force. Depending on which officers were there, the situation might not be as bad as it looked.

But if it's Dwight D or Bill Davis over there, a logical voice in my mind asked, *why would they have their flashers on? To welcome you home?*

The tow-truck driver spoke his first words to me since western New York: "You said you didn't steal this car. I wouldn'a' driven you if I thought you stole it."

"I didn't steal it," I said. It was more of a reflex than a true denial; suddenly the question of which Auburn police officer was at the museum was of paramount importance. Solving this small mystery would keep me from the larger, more stressful mystery of why police were at the museum at all.

"That *is* Dwight D's car," I said. Out of the corner of my eye, I noticed the driver staring at me. "He was my senior prom date." He shook his head and mumbled something I didn't hear as he pulled the truck into the Museum's gravel parking lot.

Dwight D appeared to be arguing with the other cop, whom I didn't recognize. When the tow-truck pulled into the lot, he turned from Dwight D and advanced on us. Dwight D stepped in front of him and the little man disappeared—Dwight D was about six-eight and seemed easily as wide as he was tall.

I opened the door before the truck had even stopped and heard the unfamiliar cop speaking to Dwight D. "—out of the way Officer Eisenhower."

I stepped around Dwight D and saw the speaker settle his belt around his waist. One hand went to his nightstick. "Dwight!" I yelled, sliding from the truck's cab. The smaller cop's head appeared in the notch between Dwight D's bent arm and his hulking torso. "It's okay."

He didn't turn around. "It's not okay, Bethany." His voice sounded oddly husky. Almost like—

I shivered. I'd never seen Dwight D scared before.

My father burst out of the museum and down the front steps. "Stop!" The bubble lights on top of the cruisers created a strobe effect and made him appear to run in jerky slow motion. "Dwight D, stop for heaven's sake!" A cell phone glowed green in his hands. "Officer Blue," he wheezed, "It's Bill—ah, Lieutenant Davis," he waved the cell phone as he ran. "The search for my daughter has been called off."

Blue eyed Dad, obviously unimpressed. Dad, oblivious, continued. "There are no charges against her." His gaze flicked to me. "So I appreciate your concern, but she can come home."

Blue grimaced and snatched the cell phone from Dad's

outstretched hand. He turned away and spoke quietly into it for a moment. He snapped Dad's cell phone closed and tossed it back to Dad. "You and the Lieutenant play bridge together?" Blue spat. "Or do all felons with Auburn addresses walk free in this town?" His voice was surprisingly low and melodic coming from so small a man.

Dad wrapped an arm around my shoulders as Blue stalked back to his car. His tires spun and sprayed gravel all over the lot as he left.

Dwight D's shoulders sagged. But his voice was still tense. "Bethany, I'd feel better if we got you out of here."

"Nonsense, Dwight D, Bill himself called off the search," Dad said. He couldn't stop rubbing my arms, as if he thought I was cold and was trying to keep me warm.

Dwight D turned to face us and suddenly I *was* cold. His eyes were glossy seashells buried deep in the sandy stubble on his cheeks.

"Is Hannah still at the café?" I hadn't even meant to speak, but now that the words were out I was glad; Dwight D regained some of his color as he considered his wife's whereabouts.

He nodded slowly.

Dad seemed ready to object again, but I said, "I could really go for some coffee. And then we could all catch up." I had some front-page news to share from my last week or so of life, and now it appeared I wasn't the only one. "Would that be alright, Dwight D?"

He breathed deeply, and was fully himself again. "She closes shop in ten minutes, but she won't mind us showing up. I know she missed seeing you at lunch," he told me.

Right…our weekly Wednesday lunch. What had I been doing Wednesday? Getting married, I thought.

The weight of the past few days crashed down on me and I suddenly felt like curling up and going to sleep. Just burying myself under a pile of blankets and hibernating for about a month.

Instead, remembering that Cliff was at the mercy of his cousin in a state mental hospital halfway across the country (the memory captured within a single penetrating rip of paper), I said, "I missed her too. Let's go."

Dad visibly swallowed any further objections and said, "Wait a second while I show the wrecker where to park."

8

Mamie's sat near the corner of Main and Jefferson, sandwiched between the town's only cobbler, The Electric Shoe, and the salon where I had earned my life's wages. The café had dark-stained wood walls and a high, carved, silvery ceiling, a relic of the early twentieth century when Main Street shops rated solid wood and shaped tin instead of sheetrock on every surface.

Hannah Eisenhower ("Mamie," as her nametag proclaimed, pinned above a large blue button that read, "I LIKE IKE"), spouse of Dwight D and as friendly and likeable as her husband was large, obviously shared her husband's concern for me; her smile was as welcoming as ever, but there was an unusual tightness around her eyes, and she hugged me a little too hard. "I'm so glad Dwight found you," she whispered. "Hello, Mr. Wray," she said more loudly when she pulled away from me. I wondered distantly if my former classmates would ever get around to calling my father by his first name. Or if my own husband would, for that matter.

Thinking so casually of Cliff brought a fresh pang of guilt that made my knees go watery and numb.

Dwight D's sharp eyes notice me wobbling and he sprang to my side with startling agility. "Hannah, can you get Bethany a large coffee please?" His huge paw was wrapped gently around my arm in support. Hannah turned toward the kitchen immediately.

"Actually we won't be staying lo—" Dad began.

"One for Dad too," I said over him, fighting to keep my voice steady. My tears seemed more eager to fall now that I was among friends again.

Dad frowned, but wisely kept further comment to himself. He sat down primly beside me.

Once the four of us were parked around one of the café's twelve round tables, nursing hot coffees (except for Dwight D, who sipped water between frequent glances at the front door), I got to ask the question that had been plaguing me since the drama in front of the museum: "What's the story with this new guy—Blue? I thought I knew all the cops in town."

"Kendall Blue," Dwight D said. "Transferred in two months ago from the Sheriff's Office. Wanted to see what it was like to keep the peace in a small town. Eric Pedersen hit the nail on the head when he called Blue 'McGruff.' The cartoon dog who tells kids how to obey the law?"

I nodded.

"Now that he's here he thinks we're all bumpkins, Bill Davis included. He filed complaint against Eric for public slander for that McGruff thing."

"So the guy's a jerk," I said. "So what?"

"Even in a town as small as Auburn, a cop who's got it in for you is bad news. Blue wouldn't have known you from Eve until tonight, but whoever called in the phony theft report and paid Blue to pick you up for it—"

My father's scorn was instant and bombastic. "Well this is the last straw, Dwight D. It really is. Police officers cannot simply be bribed to charge random civilians with absurd crimes, regardless of how cliquish or unprofessional their colleagues may be."

"Dad!"

He didn't even pause. "Now I appreciate how difficult it must have been to stand up to one of your own at the museum tonight, and I thank you for your efforts. But if you have no better rationale than this for stuffing my daughter in the back of your car like some petty criminal then we'll bid you both goodn—"

"Shut up!" I yelled. "Why are you being such a dick?"

Dwight D had taken the lashing calmly—far better, in fact, than Hannah, whose eyes glittered above harsh rosy anger spots in her cheeks—meeting my father's words with a straight back. Before Hannah or I could strike any further at my father, though, Dwight D said softly, "How *did* Blue know Bethany would come home tonight?"

Dad had opened his mouth, probably to rebuke me for my profanity, but no words came at first. Bright red hives crept up out of his collar, as if feeding off the blood draining from his face. This was a night for rare emotions: Dwight D Eisenhower had been (and still was, to judge from those glances at the door) nervous, and now my father, David Excelsior Wray, was embarrassed.

"How did he know about the Duesenberg?" Dwight D asked. "I assume you didn't report your own daughter for grand theft auto."

"Of course I didn't," Dad snapped. The hives continued their inexorable climb up his neck.

"So someone *else* knew," Dwight D coaxed, his voice still soft, but gentler. He turned to me. "When did you call your dad?"

"Yesterday morning," I said. I didn't like where this was going. "Did you tell anyone?" I asked Dad before Dwight D could.

Dad rested his elbows on the table and ran a hand down his

face. The hives were up to his ears.

I remembered handing our marriage license to Eleanor in Cliff's hospital room. The ripping sound that froze my blood even as my heart warmed at seeing Cliff open his eyes. The three others at the table blurred as those damn eager tears swam up again. "It's okay, Dad, it's not your fault." I jammed a knuckle at the bridge of my glasses and willed the tears away.

His voice was husky. "She sounded worried. Now that Alice is gone, after all, Cliff is her responsibility and I just thought..." he trailed off.

My anger flared again. I *bet* she was worried. Worried that Cliff might slip right through her slippery red scales and obsidian claws. Worried that she might be robbed of her full, pointless revenge despite his one protector being out of the picture.

"I almost didn't come out to the museum," Dwight D continued musingly, almost to himself. "Blue received a call at his desk earlier tonight, and immediately called Lieutenant Davis. Someone had reported her car stolen by a 'Beth Carlson.' I didn't see the connection to Bethany until I heard the description of the car."

Dad sighed. But he didn't seem surprised. On the contrary, his expression said the story was making perfect sense to him. "Bill didn't say anything about that," he murmured. "Was this caller who I think it was?" he asked more loudly.

I felt my eyes widening. It seemed they would grow until my eyeballs popped right out of their sockets to hang in midair from stringy nerve tissue like Wile E. Coyote witnessing an especially asinine punchline to one of his own roadrunner traps.

"Idiot!" I yelled, and pounded the table.

My father winced

Dwight D frowned. "He really couldn't have known, Bethany."

Hannah still looked ready to call him worse after his tirade against her husband.

"Not him," I said. "Me. *I'm* the idiot." The tears were finally gone, buried under an avalanche of fresh anger. Even in Marguerite's senseless hatred of Cliff, I hadn't been able to see why she would sic the cops on me. What Dad had said a second ago triggered it: *Now that Alice is gone...* Yes, Marguerite was Cliff's new legal guardian, but there was no way Alice had been mentally sick enough to will all of her money to Marguerite along with her son. Alice had known that as soon as he turned 18 next Monday he would be able to move wherever he wanted and live comfortably on the millions of dollars she was leaving behind. In that case, Marguerite probably wouldn't see a dime of her sister's money. Coming after Cliff made perfect sense. But her coming after *me* meant...

"Eleanor must've told her we got married!" I said.

My brain, realizing too late that discretion was the better part of valor, shut down all circuits to my mouth, which hung slack in the realization of what had just come barreling out—the bombshell I'd just dropped on my best friends and, even worse, my father.

Dwight D stared openly, front door forgotten for the moment.

Dad peered at me from under bunched eyebrows. "What?" he whispered.

Hannah just wore this funny knowing smile. "I wondered," she said.

I took a deep breath. "I'd better explain that, huh?"

9

Dwight D dropped Dad and me back off at the museum around one. As my story in Mamie's had progressed, he had checked the door less and less often until, when I described standing behind a two-way mirror condemning my two young hoodlums, he had abandoned his vigil altogether and listened with a child's solemn attention.

My father had kept silent since I mentioned being married. Or blurted it. His tight-lipped "Good night, Dwight D" was the first time he'd spoken since asking if Officer Blue's caller had been Marguerite.

"Do you want to get the Model J inside before we go home?" I asked. The tow truck driver had simply dumped it in the gravel lot before (gratefully, I'm sure) taking off.

"That can wait until morning," he said. A sure sign, if I needed one, that he was distraught under his veneer of calm silence.

The interior of his BMW smelled just as it had a week ago—a *lifetime* ago—as every car he'd ever owned smelled: brand new. Suddenly I was ten years old again, awaiting chastisement for riding my bike into the garage instead of walking it; for running in the museum; for using original Armor All on a leather interior at the museum. And I knew we weren't going straight home.

Dad did all his disciplining from behind the wheel. It had been that way for as long as I could remember and it would be that way now, at 25.

But Dad didn't break his silence until he pulled into our garage at home. "Tomorrow will you be able to prep the Duesenberg inside and out?" he asked, staring at his lap. The lines around his mouth and at the corners of his eyes seemed deeper than they had at the café, as if someone had traced them with a charcoal pencil.

"Okay?" I said, not sure myself if I was answering his question or posing one of my own.

"I would like to get it back in the showroom tomorrow morning. Goodnight."

He exited the car, still avoiding eye contact, and stepped stiffly through the garage/house door I had escaped from a week ago.

Then it hit me: I was no longer ten years old, and I had done a lot more than use the wrong upholstery protectant.

10

A quick glimpse into Dad's bedroom on my way down the hall then next morning showed a spotless floor and freshly made bed. Several boxes of cereal and two different kinds of bagels rested on the island in the kitchen. The coffee pot was half empty, but Dad had left it heating for me.

Had he gone to the museum without me? No matter how upset he was, Dad wouldn't ever leave me behind when he had asked me to work for him.

Well, I would not let him guilt me or worry me into rushing off to the museum on foot, arriving late and sweaty and apologetic. I popped two halves of an onion bagel into the toaster. And just to assure myself that Dad wasn't dictating my schedule, I fried up two eggs to garnish the bagels.

Halfway through my second egg and mustard bagel, Dad stepped into the kitchen from the garage. Seeing him, despite all my efforts, I did feel guilty. He was still in his jogging sweats—though my father had never jogged so much as a quarter mile in his life—and a damp green cloth hung from his hand. *The* Cloth, in fact. He had probably fifty of them stashed in a drawer in the garage, these "miracle" strips of fabric that purportedly could shine up anything from a brass trinket to an oak cabinet to a

Cadillac limousine.

"Finally awake, are you?" he said cheerfully. "No harm no foul. The car was filthy." He pitched The Cloth into a hamper under the sink. "And anyway, I couldn't bear to wake you, you looked so peaceful sleeping."

A lie; I thrashed like a tiger shark on a harpoon in my sleep. But his words made me feel worse yet. What kind of daughter was I to suspect my own father of the juvenile spite I had imagined earlier?

"We've got work today, though. Why don't you finish your breakfast and get dressed. I want the Duesenberg on the floor by noon."

I finally checked the digital clock on the stove behind me: eight o'clock. Two hours after Dad was normally at work. I pushed the rest of my sandwich away. "I'll be ready in five minutes."

Standing under the morning sky, July sun promising a real barbeque by afternoon, I decided it was good to be home. Having Cliff beside me would have completed the feeling of homecoming, but smelling the rusty railroad tracks and dusty weeds in the gravel lot, I knew this was where I belonged, not halfway across the country on the run from phantom relatives.

I eased onto the burning bench seat in the Model J and caught Cliff's scent before the other stronger odor of hot leather overpowered it. But that brief odor was enough to draw a hard lump into my throat.

No, I thought suddenly. I had decided Dad was not going to guilt me (I still vaguely wondered when this morning's calm would end and the imminent storm would come), and there was no reason I should let the memory of Cliff do so either. I had not abandoned him. The only way to help him now was to appeal to Marguerite. *That* was why I was here—not because I was running, and certainly not because I didn't care about him.

I turned the key and bore my foot savagely down on the starter pedal. There was a thin black strip of asphalt leading from Dad's single-stall pressure washer to the wide door on the back of the museum. I pulled onto that strip and nosed the Model J into the washing stall. Dad had given me a chamois before retreating into the museum's air conditioning. Everything else I needed for exterior cleaning was right in the stall: a self-soaping brush with nonabrasive bristles; a multi-pressure water gun (Dad didn't believe in any wax or wheel cleaner that could be sprayed from a pressure hose); polishing rags; several green Cloths in their own individual Ziploc baggies, just in case I came across a pesky bug or dollop of hard sap that did not yield to the pressure hose; even an extra chamois.

I tore into the job, soaping the car, rinsing, and soaping and rinsing again. I used the first chamois on the body, including the doorjambs and front and rear fenders (the leather trunk which was normally strapped above the rear fender now sat on the blacktop outside the stall, safely away from my spraying; the four straps to hold it in place reached limply from the rear of the car like the tentacles of a sleeping octopus). The second chamois dried the wheels, tires, and under the side running boards. Dad normally displayed the Model J with its engine compartment closed, so I did no cleaning under the hood. Anyway, if he did want to show off the enormous Straight 8 Eagle, he would most likely want to clean it himself.

I dried my bare feet with a chamois before entering the cockpit, hearing Dad's stern, proper voice blaring from the past as I did so.

Every extra touch you can add, Bethany, every little thing you can think of, do it. Those efforts are the difference between maintaining a car and treating one. And that's what we do: we treat cars. We have to.

I opened the glove compartment and removed the bottle of BMW brand liquid wax that Dad kept in every car in the museum. I had miles to go before the Model J was ready for the floor. I lost myself in the work.

"Stunning," Dad pronounced after his inspection. "Did you

shine the studs on the trunk straps?" he said, bending down.

"Chrome cleaner and Q-Tips," I said.

He said nothing, but I could see his chest puff up with pride as he stood. "Let's check the interior."

I opened the driver's side door with a Cloth, taking care not to let my fingers touch any part of the handle or door, and stepped aside like a chauffer as Dad peered inside. These parade ground formalities were as familiar and comfortable as sleeping at night and waking in the morning.

"Seats...check. Steering wheel...check. Pedals...check."

Dad never tired of this progression. I waited for the punchline, which could only be delivered while inspecting a Duesenberg because they were all equipped with an—

"Altimeter...check." Dad turned and grinned. I smiled dutifully back.

He straightened up again. "Fantastic work. This is the best attention to detail I have seen. José and Allain will have a new standard to meet."

I hadn't realized I was holding my breath, but I wasn't surprised when I sighed and the pressure left my chest. I wasn't sure if I'd ever made it through one of Dad's showroom inspections with an open airway.

Dad clapped me on the shoulder. "Bravo. I believe you have earned yourself some lunch."

The grandfather clock behind the yellow roadster read 1: 15. Suddenly I was famished. "Hannah only serves lunch for another fifteen minutes," I said. "We'd better get—"

Some unrecognizable emotion flashed behind Dad's eyes. "Is something wrong?" I asked.

"No," he said quickly. "But my only daughter has returned home. I think we can kill a fatter calf than Mamie's Café."

11

I was used to Dad's demands for perfection in everything pertaining to the museum, but there was a new twist: he paid me. I had wanted for nothing growing up—of course it helped that I asked for very little as far as material goods went—and for this luxury Dad had always expected hard work at the museum. If I wanted money of my own, he said, I could get a job on the side, which I eventually did at the salon. Working without pay, Dad was fond of saying, built character. According to him, so many activities at the museum built character that Allain, the former Quebecois who served as curator whenever my dad was absent, had blown up a Calvin and Hobbes cartoon wherein Calvin dons his father's glasses and mocks him by saying, "Calvin, go do something you hate. Being miserable builds character," and taped the strip on the inside of Dad's office door.

Now, though, Dad apparently believed I had built enough character, because he tripled my hourly pay from the salon. And he took me to Fort Wayne for lunch everyday. At first I just thought he was overly relieved that I had come back home. But I noticed we never talked about the week I was gone, or about my marriage, or about Cliff. In fact I never talked at all. Dad simply spouted small talk in an attempt to fill the dull emptiness

I created around me everywhere I went.

Even worse, our lunches prevented me from seeing Hannah, the only other person who could help me sort out my plan to get Cliff back.

Well, maybe not *prevented*. If I were truthful with myself, I would have to admit that thinking about going back to Maine, or even driving across town to talk to Marguerite made me so emotionally tired that I was already one day away from the weekend and I still hadn't even called the municipal building in Coldwater for a new marriage license.

Working for Dad was intoxicating; I could concentrate hard enough on cleaning cars and sweeping out corners of the various showrooms that I could ignore the voice of my quiet, exhausted conscience whispering about my responsibility to Cliff.

Friday, staring at my dad across a plate of Red Robin's famous bottomless steak fries, my bubble of false serenity popped.

"I don't know when the museum has looked better," Dad said. "I mean that. Amanda—she's the new one at the ticket counter— said more customers have…um, have told her…Bethany, are you okay? You look ill."

The cautious, prim concern in his voice made me hate him right then. It was an unfair emotion, of course. I was the only one to blame for allowing him to lull me to sleep with work and his nervous companionship. I was the one who had turned my back on the man I married. I was the one—

"You don't love him."

Another bubble popped, this time audibly. It was as if I had been floating in a sensory deprivation tank and someone pitched a rock right through the glass. Suddenly the restaurant was a chaos of sound: the clink of flatware on plates; TV announcers commenting on the Pittsburgh Pirates' chances for the pennant; a fluttery giggle from two tables behind me; a man in an expensive-looking suit on a cell phone told the person on the other end of the line, "…bump that asshole down to the loading bay, boss's son or not."

But over it all, my dad's words rolled and echoed.

You don't love him.

You don't love him.

You don't love him.

"Shut up!"

Conversation around us lulled a moment, but the only person who actually looked at me was the man on his cell phone who was planning to demote his boss's son. I glared at him until he turned back to his steak.

"Kindly lower your voice, young lady," Dad whispered fiercely. "And you will not speak to me that way either in public or in our own—"

"Excuse me, but *you* are the one who is out of line." Despite my anger I heeded him and spoke quietly. "You have no idea what I have gone through in the last two weeks, and until you care to hear about it, *I* will not be spoken to that way."

Stalemate. We sat in brooding silence until the check arrived.

"I know why you did it," Dad said as he pulled the BMW onto I-69 North. Neither of us had spoken a word since Red Robin. He sighed. "And in a way I'm proud of you."

He meant this as a compliment, but I could see where he was going. I decided to let him say it out loud before my fury took over.

"As a parent you never know how your children will handle morally demanding situations," he continued.

Okay, never mind letting him finish. "You think I married Cliff out of charity, is that it?" I marveled at how quiet my voice was. Actually it scared me a little; I should have been screaming.

Dad peered at me over the tops of his tiny circular glasses, eyebrows reaching for his hairline as if to say, "Well?"

Now I would yell and scream. Surely. This patronizing look was the last straw. My mouth unhinged and I waited eagerly for the cutting words to flow out.

Eventually Dad turned back to the road, smug that he had hit so close to the mark that I was speechless.

The real answer is even worse, my conscience whispered.
*That's why I'm sitting here with my mouth hanging open wide
enough to attract flies and nothing's coming out.*

The seams in the highway streamed under the car hypnotically.
Ka-CLACK, Ka-CLACK, Ka-CLACK.

"No," I said. Not to Dad, but to the voice in my own head.
My fingertips and teeth had gone numb.

Dad shrugged, clearly accepting my initial silence as
vindication enough to drop the subject for the moment.

"Why do you hate him?" I suddenly asked. I had hoped the
accusation would make my anger come back and wash away the
numbness, but as soon as I'd said it I felt even worse.

"That's a silly question and you know it," he said.

I nodded, holding back tears. I hadn't cried as much in my
whole life as I had in the last two weeks. *Because I love him.
Right?*

"Bethany, I'd—" His hands tightened on the wheel, making
the leather creak. "I had always hoped you would find someone
who shared our..." he twirled a hand in the air, "...appreciation,
I suppose, of fine cars. People have offered me such asinine
amounts of money for the museum that I could go kick Bill
Gates off his island and still have hundred dollar bills for my
new fireplace."

He cleared his throat. "But that's not the point."

"I know," I said, so softly he didn't hear me.

"If you had come home with a ring from Allain—" (Dad
had been pushing from both sides for this to happen since
the Canadian had shown up in Auburn three years ago) "—or
José—"

"José is sixteen years old!" (That Cliff was would only turn
eighteen next Monday conveniently did not occur to me.)

"—or even that ox Dwight D, I would have been overjoyed.
They know what the museum means to us."

I remembered telling Cliff I would "take or leave" most of the cars in the museum, but that hadn't been exactly true. If Dad or I saw a fingerprint or nose smudge from an overly-enthusiastic visitor on any window of any car in the museum it would be a race to see which of us got there first with the Windex.

Another memory surfaced. My chest hitched and a loud sob almost like the bark of a big dog escaped me. "He was so proud, Dad. He was so proud of his stupid Toyota Corolla." I was really crying now, harder than I had at the Bangor Mental Health Institute. "He had as many cleaning supplies for that one car as we have for a whole room of them at the museum." Unstable laughter mixed with my tears. "He had to buy darker sunglasses because of the glare off his dashboard. You could almost see your reflection in the vinyl."

Dad frowned. "Home car maintenance is one thing—"

"And she took his car away."

"Who?"

"That's why I left, Dad. I couldn't let her win one more time. They were going to put him in a mental hospital."

I could see Dad squaring up to tell me Cliff *was* in a mental hospital, but I pressed on before he could. I wasn't sure how I would respond if he got out that little nugget.

"That's why I've buried myself in museum chores since coming home. I didn't have to think about how I turned Cliff's life upside down not because I loved him, but because I wanted revenge on Marguerite.

"And because…" Here it was. The five words I had been afraid to say because I thought if I said them aloud they might sound too true and they would soil my relationship with Cliff forever after. "I felt sorry for him."

There. I waited for my stomach to clench. I waited for my mind to examine the last three years of my life through the metaphorical bifocals of those five words, and declare that there was, in fact, nothing else to my feelings for Cliff. Just a good old case, albeit modified, of the Florence Nightingale effect.

"Don't be silly," my father said. "Only a blind man could

miss the way you change when you talk about that boy. Or a very stubborn one," he added more softly.

"But—"

"Yes, yes, five minutes ago I said the opposite," Dad said, waving his hand dismissively. "I didn't mind hating myself for trying to keep you at home." He sighed. "I never thought it would work."

He dropped one hand to the gear shift and the other clutched the steering wheel at about eleven o'clock: his posture for making a speech. "I have made some lousy choices in the past weeks, Bethany. Working you like a drone at the museum and letting your doubt fester are the latest, if not the worst." His eyes never left the road. "I ask you to forgive me, Bethany. I don't know if you should, but I ask it anyway."

The clacking of the highway seams took over again.

"I have to leave again."

"I know."

12

The BMW blew past the Auburn exit at 80 miles per hour. "Um, Dad? We not going home?"

In the last fifteen minutes the atmosphere between Dad and me had been more amicable than anytime since I had come back from Maine.

He ignored my question. "Why were you in Maine anyway?" he asked. "You never told us that."

Dry brown and yellow fields, recovering from the recent harvest, flashed past my window. Stiff trees, planted in long rows to keep the topsoil from blowing away on windy days, swayed not an inch in the calm July heat.

"I don't know," I said. "That was Cliff's idea." I remembered the passion that flooded Cliff's eyes in the hotel when he told me where we were going. He had seemed very strong right then. "He wanted to go to Prince Edward Island."

"I lied to you," I said suddenly, remembering how I'd told him we were in Chicago, hoping he would tell Marguerite and throw her off our trail.

"Yes."

A thousand words (excuses, more like) clamored at the tip of my tongue. I forced them back. "I'm sorry."

Dad sighed again and then sniffed deeply. "There's nothing like 'I'm sorry' for apologizing," he said.

Only my father could utter this type of absurdity with any semblance of gravity. At the risk of ruining our self-flagellation—not that I was really in control of my emotions right now—I giggled.

The clouds over his brow broke and he burst out laughing. "I love your laugh," he said. "It's a happy sound." He grew more serious. "I've missed that sound since you're back."

He clapped a hand on my knee. "Before either one of us apologizes again, let's just say we've both been a couple of shitheads and move on already."

"Dad!" I said, incredulous.

"Well?"

"Yeah."

By the time we stepped out of the Henry L. Brown Municipal Building, fresh marriage license in hand, the building's formidable stone facade was in the shadow of the setting sun. A question occurred to me. "Dad?"

"Hmm?"

"Why were you talking to Marguerite while I was gone?"

Dad paused midstride. "I know I made a lot of mistakes, Bethany. And before we get into another apologizing match, let me say I'm sorry for all of those mistakes right now."

I curled an arm around his neck. "I don't think either of us wants to remember the way we handled our affairs that week," I said. "But I'm not looking for a confession or repentance. I really want to know. It might help Cliff."

Dad frowned, but in remembrance rather than irritation. "Let's see, you called Friday afternoon, is that right?"

I did the mental math. I had gotten home Sunday night, after two and-a-half grueling days trapped in the silent, pungent tow-truck. "Yeah."

"Then I called Marguerite. I asked if her daughter was out of the hospital yet. As far as I knew, we were just two single parents with children in trouble."

I remembered Eleanor reaching for our new marriage license in another hospital. Her left hand held protectively across the stomach of her ever-present jean jacket, wrapped in that ridiculous pink cast. The only name on that cast had been her own, written in several different styles and colors. What had she done to earn that cast?

I tried hard not to pity her.

"Obviously a mistake," he said, disgusted. "But she told me that now, in addition to Cliff, her daughter…"

"Eleanor," I reminded him.

He nodded. "She was gone too now. As far as I could tell, we were two single parents with runaway children. She told me to get back to her if I heard anything."

"She's the one who sent Eleanor to find us!" I nearly yelled in the parking lot. But I wasn't angry at Dad anymore; Marguerite's ability to manipulate had put a pen in her sister's dying hand to sign her son into the custody of a woman who had nearly killed him as a baby.

Dad shrugged. "She didn't say that." He pressed his keychain remote to unlock the BMW and disarm its alarm. "I told her you would probably be back Sunday evening."

"Then on Sunday?" I prompted.

"Officer Blue showed up maybe a half-hour before you did, and I assumed he was there to collect Cliff. As far as I knew, they were still after him for your kidnapping." He paused, probably making sure I wouldn't yell again. When I stayed silent, he continued. "Dwight D arrived shortly after. He was so angry, I worried they might come to blows."

"Dwight D could've tossed him over the museum with one hand," I said.

"That's exactly what I was afraid he'd do," Dad said. "And I doubted the law would favor him if he did. So I called Bill Davis at his home and told them Cliff wasn't even with you."

His mouth turned down in a grim line. "He said *you* were the one they were after, for grand theft auto. He must have seen through the name before Dwight D did." He glanced over at me. "It's a good thing you took the car you did."

I shivered. Good thing indeed. The Model J was one of five cars in the whole museum that Dad actually owned, even though he showed many of them. One of the museum's donors most likely would not have been as forgiving as Dad at my putting almost two thousand miles on his million-plus dollar car.

"I was worried about you, Bethany. After Marguerite called and told me Cliff had attacked her and run off, on top of finding your note that you were with him, I wanted you back home more than I have ever wanted anything. But I did not tell Marguerite that you took a car from the museum." His eyes were wide. "Do you believe me?"

I squeezed his arm. "Of course I believe you." I knew what Marguerite was capable of. Turning my Dad's natural fear for me to her advantage must have been like shooting fish in a barrel.

"I can't come into the museum tomorrow," I said aloud.

"Tomorrow's Saturday," he said. "I probably won't go in either."

Saturday. A heavy steel ball, like a shot-put, dropped into my stomach as I registered once more that I had been emotionally asleep for a week. What terrors had Cliff experienced in these five days?

"I'm not leaving yet—I need to talk to Hannah."

13

Mamie's was always a zoo at lunchtime. Plates clattered back in the kitchen, the old fashioned cash register chugged and clanged like an antique steam engine with a bell instead of a whistle. The espresso machine gurgled and screamed at the chore of steam-heating milk for the next latte. Noises of chewing and talk rolled upward like calm surf and broke against the tin ceiling, punctuated occasionally by a high laugh or a sneeze.

Hannah thrived on this symphony. It was the music of summer, she had told me once. Only people in shorts and tank tops sounded like this. Sweaters and corduroy slacks had their own comforting allure in the winter, but nothing, she said, compared to the joy of being half naked in public.

She sat across from me, fingers laced around a mug of coffee. I told her first of the conversation with my dad yesterday.

"Good," she said. "He was being a total prig the other night." But her voice held the gentle exasperation of forgiving a silly old friend.

"Listen, you and Dwight didn't get to say much after, well…" I glanced around the café self-consciously.

"After you blew up the world with your marriage bomb?" Hannah said loudly, an impish smile on her face.

I glanced around again, instinctively ducking my head. I hadn't seen anyone I knew in the café yet, but that meant little in a town like Auburn, especially with my father's near-celebrity status.

I nodded.

"The part you're not telling me," she said, "is how scared you are that you married Cliff for the wrong reason." She was still talking at normal volume, but I straightened up, a strange tingling in my cheeks and on the back of my neck. She cocked an accusing eyebrow at me. "Stop pretending to be surprised. The only time we haven't been best friends in the last ten years is when you stole Dwight for the prom."

"How else was I going to be prom queen?" I said, finishing our old joke. "Everyone was too scared of him *not* to vote me in."

But the joke wasn't funny today. I had liked Dwight D well enough, but the truth was I *had* known nobody would vote against him

"Oh boy," Hannah sighed. "You sure know how to torture yourself. Bethany, do you remember a couple years ago when Cliff brought that hideous tan car here for the first time?"

Now it was my turn to frown at her.

"I was in here, but I saw you guys outside." She stirred her coffee restlessly with her index finger. When she looked back up her eyes locked on mine. "I had planned on dying without telling you this because it's stupid and unfair, but I was actually jealous of Cliff right then. I knew that I—your best friend for a decade—could never say or do anything that would make you as happy as you were plopped down on the curb beside him staring at a cheap sedan."

The finger dipped back into her coffee. "I figured something had happened to Cliff when you stopped showing up for lunch. And when Dwight D called me here on Sunday, saying you were going to be picked up for grand theft auto…That's why Dwight was worried. Bad cops, cops on the take—pick any B movie cliché you want. All he knew was that something was rotten in Denmark."

"Marguerite," I breathed, my lip curling. A vision of Jerry Seinfeld popped into my mind, his own upper lip disappearing as he uttered the name of his own nemesis, as if cursing: "*Newman.*"

Hysterical laughter nearly bubbled out of my throat to add to the "summer music" in the café before I put a hasty clamp on my jaw.

Hannah had lifted her mug to drink, but set it back down. "Listen to me, Bethany. We all have our private suspicions, but the truth is you are safe at home. If there was anything untoward, it disappeared the instant your dad told Bill you had his car, not some piece of stolen museum merchandise."

Her message was obvious: *Everything worked out. Drop it and be happy, because this could make the Auburn cops look pretty bad. And when police have a grudge against you, your life can go straight to hell faster than you can say "sullied reputation."*

I felt a bitter, angry smile still on my lips. Hannah recoiled from my expression, but I could not change it. "Cliff has experienced more offense in the last month than I have in my whole life, and it's still going on."

Her hazel eyes widened in hurt. " No…I didn't mean—"

"I know, Hannah." Just like the time I passed out on the bench seat of the Model J in Maine, sudden exhaustion washed over me, making my whole body feel stiff and slow and old, like cotton had been packed tightly into every joint. "And I appreciate your advice; it's much wiser than I could do on my own right now. I just can't follow it."

Relief replaced the hurt I had seen. "Dwight agreed with me that you wouldn't listen to any of that. But he asked me to say it anyway." A new ferocity came across her features. "For what it's worth, you have the largest lawman and the most beautiful restaurateur in Auburn for your backup in whatever you do next."

A bizarre image came to my mind: stark white hands reaching out from black dusty bushes. I remembered being afraid of those hands. Then the whole dream returned, all at once: the cracked femur; the silky blue smoke and ash; the silent, gorgeous red dragon with its hard golden eyes. I wasn't looking forward to marching into her cave.

"As long as we're talking about family, are you going to Alice's memorial service on Monday?" Hannah asked. Her finger was once again submerged in her coffee.

"Wait. Cliff's *mom* Alice?"

Hannah nodded. "I know it'll be hard, but I'll come if you want me to, and Dwight D. Your dad's probably going too, isn't he?"

"She died almost two weeks ago," I said numbly.

"They usually do it sooner than that, don't they?" Hannah said, frowning. "Maybe the autopsy results took a long time?"

"She died of advanced skin cancer," I said. "There wouldn't have been any autopsy."

No, Marguerite had waited two weeks for a different reason—Monday was Cliff's eighteenth birthday.

14

Heat doesn't own the northern Indiana summer, but it shows up on our doorstep and makes us sweat every couple weeks like a trucker checking in with one of his families-on-the-side. *Hey, hey. Kids alright? Wow, Susie's sure growing up. Bought you a puppy. Well, gotta run.*

Today was his visiting day, and St. Mark's Episcopal Church had no air conditioning. Half the town fanned themselves in the unpadded wooden pews, melting in their heavy black suits, but determined to pay Alice Carlson their last respects. Dad and Hannah sat on either side of me. Dwight D was also there, towering over Hannah's left side. Allain and José sat on the other side of Dad. I had never seen José wearing anything besides corduroy shorts and a death metal t-shirt (most commonly advertising Skid Row and Limp Bizkit), and maybe he never *had* worn anything else; he tugged awkwardly at his white collar every few seconds and kept loosening his tie until the knot hung down below the second button on his shirt. When he noticed me watching him he grinned and extended his index finger and pinky in the universal sign for the devil's horns. Definitely his first memorial service. In contrast, Allain's face was as proper and serene as ever above his dapper black double-breasted suit and below his styled Harry Connick Jr. hair.

I allowed myself a grateful smile at this entourage. This really was home, and these people were my family.

Well, most of it.

Aside from the conspicuous absence of the deceased's only child, Alice herself was not present. There was no casket up front; she had been in the ground since two days after she died, according to the program which now served as a limp fan for most of the congregation.

Also, I had not yet seen Marguerite or Eleanor. I had marched us up to the second row of pews, obeying a stiff-necked instinct that I belonged with the other two members of Alice's family who would attend. I was her daughter-in-law, dammit, even if she hadn't known it. I was here representing Cliff as well as myself. Except for that last ugliness in Alice's hospital room—which, if I was honest, was as much my fault as hers, and perhaps more because I wasn't dying—I had respected and loved her as the mother I had been lacking for the last twenty years.

Marguerite glided out from a side door and planted herself behind the pulpit. She looked absolutely stunning. Her dress was green velvet rather than black, but the green was so dark that when she shifted to view the different sides of the congregation, parts of the dress appeared black. She should have been glistening with sweat in that gown, but she appeared neither wet nor dry. Her flawless cheeks and bare arms were the perfect shade of fair to compliment her shining hair, which was in turn the perfect shade of dark red to compliment her dress, which complimented her skin, and around and around in a spiral of aesthetic perfection that was hypnotizing. An almost melodramatic hush fell over the congregation at her entrance—the papery whisper of people fanning themselves all but stopped.

I shivered with inadequacy, in that moment knowing completely how Eleanor must have felt her whole life every time she so much as glanced at her mother.

How am I going to do this?

"Welcome, and thank you all for coming," Marguerite said softly into the microphone. Her alto voice was the aural counterpart to her appearance, mellow and intoxicating. "We are here today to remember my sister, Alice Carlson." She swept her brilliant green-gold eyes over the whole assembly. "More importantly, we are here to celebrate her life."

I scanned down the program for probably the tenth time, my gaze stopping near the bottom on the portion of the service that read, "Words from Friends." The program didn't say who those "Friends" would be, which was lucky; the fewer people who knew I wasn't supposed to go up there, the better.

"As if the sadness of losing a member of our small family and town were not enough, there are other challenges today. My daughter Eleanor is unable to be here, but with good reason," she paused, again raking the congregation with her dizzying eyes.

But I was not dizzy this time. I wanted to hear this part. *Needed* to. If she said what I thought she would, maybe my righteous courage would come back to me.

"As many of you might or might not know, Alice's son, Cliff, struggled deeply with the grief of his mother's passing, and is temporarily in a hospital for his own protection. That is the main reason for the delay of this service."

So that's your spin. Keep talking, Aunt Marge. Keep feeding my resolve.

"He wants you all to know he is alright, but hopes you understand his need to deal with this issue within the family. He asked Eleanor to be with him while the town remembers and celebrates his mother. I am sure the difficulty for him is especially keen, as today is his eighteenth birthday."

This time sighs and gasps accompanied her visual sweep of the congregation, as if eye contact was maintaining her spell. And why wouldn't it? What evidence did anyone here have— second row excluded—that everything Marguerite said was not truthful. It was a desperate picture she painted, but a hopeful and beautiful one too.

"Before she left," Marguerite continued, "my daughter created a slideshow of our family's favorite pictures." A wide white projection screen began lowering silently behind Marguerite. "Hopefully it will show you exactly what family meant to my sister."

Eleanor's ability to string photographs together to tell a story was impressive, as was the music she looped behind the pictures. I knew Alice well enough to know how disgusted she would have been with sappy classical music like Pachabel's Canon in D, designed to make people cry at weddings and funerals. Eleanor had picked Dave Brubeck's rendition of "Maria" from *West Side Story*, and a very old recording of the Count Basie Orchestra playing "Just a Closer Walk with Thee," two of Alice's favorites.

I doubt even the most stiff-lipped in the congregation got through five bars of Paul Desmond's alto saxophone solo before breaking down. The first image was of Alice and Marguerite vamping at the camera wearing huge sunglasses, halter tops, and big floppy pony tails in the stands at a NASCAR race. In the next, the sisters looked about the same, except their hair had changed, and each had a baby perched on her hip, Cliff wearing a too-large yellow sun hat, Eleanor still chubby and cute in a baby sombrero.

And so it went: mostly Alice and Cliff (Eleanor unobtrusively leaping over about six months of Cliff's life when any picture of him would have shown ugly bruises on his back and face—that is, I realized, if there *were* any pictures from that time) together at home; one hilarious picture of a five-year-old Cliff reaching up toward the camera with a wide-eyed expression of horror on his face, a busy classroom behind him and a young teacher reeling him toward the other students—the infamous Miss Aloe about whom Alice had laughingly told me.

My heart stopped. Cliff in front of my salon, smiling nervously. I remembered Alice's proud, grateful features as she handed me a twenty-dollar bill for a haircut that cost just over half that. I heard my own voice telling them my name and the ironic echo of what I would tell Cliff in the hospital parking lot two years later. "Bethany," I'd said. "I'm always here."

The slide changed again. Soon enough Cliff stood proudly in front of his beige Corolla, and Alice's hand giving him the thumbs-up just visible on the left side of the frame. Hannah emitted a choked laugh beside me.

After about ten minutes of this, on the final shimmering chord of "Just a Closer Walk with Thee," Alice, Cliff, Eleanor, and Marguerite, the last of the Carlsons (*Besides me*, I amended with vicious passion), waved at the camera from Epcot Center. The kids were probably twelve. Alice wore a Goofy hat with giant buck teeth sticking out from the bottom of the hat's bill, her mouth wide open in a hearty laugh at Cliff, whose head was turned nearly backwards on his neck to get a good look at Epcot's trademark geodesic ball.

The lights came up amid muted laughter, heavy sniffs, and even some applause. When Marguerite took the pulpit again, her eyes were puffy and her mascara had run around her eyes. Neither of these lessened her beauty, however. "Pastor Sanborn, who baptized Cliff and Eleanor, and actually married Alice and Ben twenty years ago, has a brief meditation and prayer."

As Pastor Sanborn spoke my mind wandered to what I would say once I was up in front of basically the town of Auburn. I could burn Marguerite down right on the spot if I wanted to. Whatever I said would make its way to the rest of the town by this afternoon, and explode outward from there in a radius that would include Fort Wayne, Ligonier, Sturgis, and Montpelier.

I could ruin her.

"...referee banned her from the field for the next three games," Arlis Lehman said into the microphone. "I'll never forget that," he chuckled, wiping his eyes.

I scanned the program for Arlis's name...nothing. This must already be "Words from Friends."

I stood and marched up to the pulpit before Arlis was even off the stage—before I knew I was going to do it, as a matter of fact. The first face I registered was Marguerite's. Her eyes were wide and I thought she might leap up and whisk me offstage before I could say a word. But she stayed where she was, not quite scowling.

Then the weight of the rest of the congregation's eyes landed and knocked the wind out of me. My knees twitched under my dress. *Imagine the audience in their underwear,* the old stage adage came to me. Immediately an image of Marguerite in a slinky dark green brassiere and panties filled my head. *Wow, she is hot,* I thought. With a slight smile that threatened to become hooting giggles, my paralysis broke.

"I hadn't planned on speaking today," I began. "But sometimes responsibility to people we love—and loved—outweighs other fears, like talking in front of people." More muted laughter, polite and heartening.

"A lot of you know my own mother passed away when I was five years old. And three years ago a new sort of mother quite literally walked into my life. You saw the picture a second ago on the screen. Cliff, in his infinite and wonderful peculiarity, decided I was the only person who could cut his hair, so he and Alice visited the salon every two weeks like clockwork. The two of them became a whole new arm of my family, which is really why I'm up here. Family. The last time I saw Alice she said her most pressing wish was that her family—her son, her sister, and her niece—would continue developing a positive relationship after she was gone."

My voice broke on the last word. Who was I trying to kid? Marguerite herself had said this service was to remember and celebrate Alice, and how was I doing that? By telling the whole town that Cliff and I had secretly married the day after she died? By telling them that underneath her sister's perfect skin there was really a sleek, red, and wholly evil dragon with hypnotizing eyes?

"Even though Alice has passed on, I hope I can continue being a part of that family."

I hurried down the steps into my pew, sucking my bottom lip up under my front teeth and trying not to release the sob welling up in my chest.

15

Cliff's old house was not the dragon's cave I'd built up in my mind. Standing on the front walkway, warm lights glowed merrily from the living- and dining room windows. Soft jazz music spilled out to the street from the back yard, probably from an open kitchen window. This could have been any summer night for the past couple years, with Cliff and Alice in the kitchen cleaning up after dinner, maybe twirling one another in a spontaneous jazz step while Alice washed and Cliff dried the dishes. There had been such joy in this house.

I could have stood there all night, listening to Cool Jazz and letting memories eddy around me until I drowned in them. I got my feet moving toward the front door, and even lifted a hand to ring the doorbell before I stopped myself. I doubted if any of the Carlsons had ever stepped through the front door, except to welcome a visitor into the house. *Family* came and went through the back door.

And that's what I am, I told myself fiercely. In spirit and in law, for better or for worse, until death do I part. Judge Barn Owl told me that himself.

I followed the limestone path Cliff and Alice had put in together right up to the back door. Family would probably just walk in, but I wouldn't carry the role too far yet. A chair scraped on the linoleum inside at the sound of my knock.

"Eleanor?" Marguerite called. It was the same voice from the service this morning, but with an ugly edge. "Why in the hell did you turn off—"

The door swung open and I saw her pupils shrink in recognition. Her body was back-lit from the kitchen, and the green had all but disappeared from her eyes. Only the gold flecks shone now, like the eyes of a deep sea fish, hunting its prey in absolute dark. I tried not to fidget or cross my arms under that stare.

The illusion passed. Graceful calm settled over her like a cloak and she was regal again, even in her old gray t-shirt and denim capris. "Come in, Bethany." She walked over to the windowsill and switched off the music.

I closed the door, determined not to let the familiar odors in the house lull me into feeling secure.

"Sit," Marguerite said, but not unkindly. When I had obeyed, she did likewise. "I want to thank you for the reserve you showed today. There has been some ugliness in our family over the last few weeks, and I am grateful that you realized there was no point in exposing it to the town."

"You were exactly right when you said the service was for remem—"

"I'm not finished." Her tone was like waking up to a glass of icy water in the face.

"Excuse me?"

"I don't know what you hoped to accomplish by your little stunt of marrying my idiot nephew, and I don't care. I am already ahead of you, and I will always be ahead of you."

"Excuse me?" I was getting to be a real broken record here, but no other words would come out.

"Alice's money is Cliff's now, which I'm sure you know. I never asked her for it because one: I don't need it, and two: she wouldn't have given it to me anyway."

"What I said today was true," I blurted. The words came out

on their own. "About Alice wanting her family to stay together after she died."

"Of course it was true." She waved a hand dismissively. "Why do you think she signed Cliff into my custody? And I have to say, taking Cliff to Michigan to marry him was very creative. I knew you wanted a piece of the action, but even I didn't see you going that far. What were you going to do for an encore if marrying him didn't work, get pregnant with his idiot child?"

Red splotches had appeared on my forearms. I imagined my face looked like a rose garden in the snow right about now. "If you say that word one more time..."

Marguerite bolted to her feet. *"Are you threatening me in my own home?"* she shrieked. She grabbed the cordless phone off of the wall. Color had worked its way into her own cheeks now too, but it only made her look braver, more resilient. She stood there for several seconds, telephone upraised in one hand, as if ready to fend me off if I went for her throat.

For my part, I simply stared at her, struggling to keep my face and posture relaxed. Despite her words, I didn't think she was the one in danger here.

"Tell you what," she said, abruptly calm again. "In two minutes I am going to lock myself in the bathroom, dial nine-one-one, and tell them someone dangerous is in my home. If you're gone when they get here I'll tell them I didn't get a good look at the person. But before you go, listen carefully: Alice left Cliff all her money, like I said. But if Cliff is for some reason incapable of dealing with said money, it goes to the next of kin. I suppose that would normally be his wife, now that he has one, but Alice's will mentions me by name."

She blinked innocently. "I'd say being in a mental hospital qualifies as being incapable of dealing with money, wouldn't you?" She tilted her head and put a finger to her chin, as if having a great epiphany. "Gee, if only he could *explain* to the hospital staff that he's not crazy." She might also have said *If only cars ran on water and shot perfume out their tailpipes,* in that dreamy tone. "That would solve a lot of his problems, wouldn't it?"

She was baiting me, and I knew it, but it still took all of my self-control not to claw her eyes out.

"And you know what else could solve his problems?" Her eyes narrowed. "You. All you have to do is annul your marriage, and Eleanor gets Cliff out of the hospital. I give Cliff his money and he can move to the Yukon and sell high-tops to Bigfoot for all I care.

"Oh, right, and there's this one other thing." She opened a drawer and drew out a piece of paper. I saw yellow and pink carbon duplicates attached. "Tomorrow you will file this restraining order with Officer Kendall Blue at the police station, and no member of the Carlson family will be able to come within one hundred yards of you for the rest of our lives. I don't know how we'll manage," she said dryly.

It was perfect. Once Cliff got home, she could show him a certified legal document claiming I wanted nothing to do with him or his family forever. And why would he bother trying to track me down? I had walked out on him in Maine, hadn't I?

"Why do you hate him so much?" I asked. I was in the loser's circle, broken and drained. "If you don't care about the money, why can't you let him be happy?"

"I'm sorry, I thought you were the one going after my dead sister's fortune. Would Cliff be happier if I let you spend all her money and *then* leave him?" Her lip curled in a sneer. "Nobody could love that dull boy besides his own mother, who I did love, no matter what you believe. I won't dirty her memory by letting you loot her estate."

"Is that why you dropped him?" I said hotly. Maybe I wasn't broken yet. Not if her self-righteous words could still make me this angry. "Because you loved your sister so much?"

"You have thirty seconds." She thumbed the *Talk* button on the phone.

"And where is Eleanor?" I asked. "You thought I was her when I knocked, didn't you? Hasn't she called? Maybe she realized what a bitch you were being toward Cliff, and helped him along his way."

"Fifteen seconds," she said calmly. But the hand wrapped around the telephone was white-knuckled and shaking.

"Don't worry, I'll get out of your house. But remember that *everything* I said today was the truth. I loved Alice like a mother, and through her eyes I saw what a beautiful person Cliff is. No matter what *you* believe, dragon, I love my husband deeply, and I will stay married to him even if we're penniless and I have to visit him in a mental hospital everyday for the next ten years." I took the blank restraining order off the kitchen table and shredded it, much as Eleanor had done with our marriage license two weeks ago. I enjoyed it.

Marguerite seemed to ponder this. Then she nodded. She began dialing, but she dialed seven numbers instead of three. "Officer Blue? This is Marguerite Carlson. Someone is…" her eyes bored into mine. "Bethany *Carlson* is trespassing in my house. She has cursed at me and threatened me with harm. Could you please come pick her up?…No, I locked myself in the bathroom…I will certainly stay here." She pressed the *Off* button. "Welcome to our family."

16

The cruiser pulled up and inched along behind me, bright spotlight illuminating my whole body and casting long shadows on the lawn next to me.

"BETH CARLSON," a deep, musical voice blared over a loud speaker.

Hannah had been right—old Blue wasn't done with me yet. I kept walking.

"YOU ARE UNDER ARREST FOR TRESPASSING AND ASSAULT. PLEASE TURN AROUND AND KEEP YOUR HANDS WHERE I CAN SEE THEM."

I turned around slowly and squinted into the spot light trying to devise a way this could end well. Blue had been embarrassed at the museum and his ego was still smarting. Guys like Blue bruised easily in that respect and took a long time to heal.

Curtains and blinds rustled in windows all along the street. People in Auburn were too adept at spying on their street to do anything as obvious as flip on a light. For every pale oval face I saw in a window, three more watched through a crack in their Venetian blinds or gauzy curtains.

Play along, I thought. *Let him have his fun.* Then my dad's voice broke in again: *Every extra touch you can add, Bethany, every little thing you can think of, do it.* He had been talking about cars, but the advice seemed sound enough in this situation.

I stepped off the curb and walked slowly toward his cruiser, my hands held way out to the sides. I heard his door open, but still saw nothing besides the nearly angelic brightness of the spotlight.

"That's far enough," he said, stepping out from the spotlight's corona.

I took one more step and, for good measure, placed my hands on the hood of his car.

"You must get arrested a lot," he said approvingly. "Does your pal Eisenhower make you bend over his car like that every time he...*arrests* you?"

One of Hannah's favorite lines popped into my head: *Is this guy for real?* After the emotional stress of the memorial service and dealing with Marguerite in her own home, Blue's juvenile mockery didn't seem "for real" at all. He was a caricature—a cartoon version of real life.

An image of McGruff the Crime Dog popped into my head. "Whenever I solve a crime," McGruff barked in his gravelly voice, "Aunty Marge gives me a bone. *Ruff!*"

"Oh, is assault funny?" Blue said.

I couldn't help it. Thank goodness for small miracles: I kept my mouth shut and didn't make any noise. But my body shook with silent laughter.

"Real funny," he said.

All of a sudden his hands were on my ankles.   "Your victim said you threatened her. Are you armed?" His hands moved with logical precision. *Slide up, squeeze. Slide up, squeeze.*

"No," I said. I wasn't laughing anymore. There was nothing sexual about his touch, just a cold, invasive efficiency that was still somehow eager. "No, I am not armed," I repeated more loudly.

"No problem," he said easily. The hands slid up between my legs and pressed into my crotch, but did not linger. Just kept their spidery pace up my body. "But I have to see for myself, don't I?"

On my butt, my hips, my sides, all the time sliding and squeezing.

"Can't have you sticking a knife through the seat while I drive you to the station," he continued in that same low, easy tone. The guy would have made a great disc jockey.

The hands slid into my armpits, between my breasts, under them, around my stomach. My arms were bare but he checked them anyway, saving my neck and hair for last. All this without even an ounce of sexuality in his touch. Just that inhuman, invasive curiosity that was somehow just as awful as if he had tried to take advantage of me.

Finally those spidery hands grabbed my shoulders and turned me to face him.

"You knew for a fact I had no weapons." I was surprised at the venom in my voice. If I had been him, I would have taken a step back from that voice.

But Blue simply straightened his uniform and said, "All I knew for a fact was that you are suspected of committing two serious crimes this evening. I'll not take my chances because you're best friends with all the rest of the cops in this town."

"If you touch any part of my body again I'll cry rape, because that's what just happened. You got away with it once, but we'll see how many of the people watching us right now would stay in their houses and let you do it again."

Blue's face darkened. "I'm just doing my job. But I'm sure you're right. It seems people in this town can't let a person do anything without sticking their noses in it." He spoke with the careful, menacing enunciation of Darth Vader. "Now get in the car."

Blue called in my arrest on our way back to the station. When we pulled up I saw Dwight D looming at the entrance like a pissed off bouncer at a club. The instant the car stopped he yanked open the back door and hauled me out. I could tell he was trying to be gentle, but my teeth clicked together and I almost stumbled when he set me on my feet. Just like I hadn't seen Dwight D scared until a week ago, I wasn't sure I'd ever seen him this angry. I didn't know which was worse.

He swung a protective arm around my neck, and I could feel his bicep tensed from the top of my head almost to the middle of my back.

One thing was certain—Blue would not be touching me again tonight.

Inside the station I allowed the tidal force that was Dwight D Eisenhower to lead me past the front desk toward Bill Davis's office.

"If you do not stop, Officer Eisenhower, I will have to file a report against you. Procedure is to place her in a holding cell—"

Dwight D whirled on the smaller man. "She has committed no crime. This is already an ugly case of harassment. I can't see why you would want to turn it into a violation of her constitutional rights."

"Oh, please," Blue spat. "I didn't even cuff her. She rode in the back seat like a movie star."

Do you feel up all the movie stars you arrest? I wanted to ask. But I kept my mouth shut.

"Although, I suppose you didn't mind breaking procedure regarding this same person in that fiasco at the other night at the museum," Dwight D said. "You'll forgive Bill if he takes a closer look at Bethany's case before he locks her up."

"*Lieutenant* Davis can look as closely as he likes, Officer."

Dwight D straightened back up without a word and continued herding me to Bill's office. Through the open door I saw a room that was closer to a parlor than an office. A desk lamp with a green glass shade cast the room's only light. The dim, almost hazy atmosphere somehow reminded me of that painting, *Dogs Playing Poker.*

Bill himself stood when he saw Dwight D ushering me through the small maze of the other officers' desks. "Bethany, come in, come in." He pulled out a chair.

Officer Blue stood at attention. "With all due respect, Lieutenant, Miss Carlson—"

"Missus," I corrected him. "I am married."

A vein stood out on his forehead. "My mistake. Missus Carlson is suspected of a crime. Perhaps we could question her in the interrogation room according to protocol."

"Kendall, I suspect your relationship with the elder Mrs. Carlson is closer to criminal behavior than whatever Bethany has done tonight. Now remain silent or don't remain at all." His eyes remained on Blue a moment longer, then flicked down to me. Despite his hefty jowls and greasy black comb-over, Bill's eyes were as sharp as ever. "What's your story?"

I took a breath. "I was over at Marguerite's house before Officer Blue picked me up."

"Why?"

"We are both trying to use the law to get Cliff where we want him, but where she wants him and where I want him are opposites. I decided to visit with her tonight to discuss this problem."

"She said you threatened her, cursed at her."

"I cautioned her not to call my husband an idiot, which she had already done several times, and unfortunately I did let my temper get the best of me—I called her a dragon and said she was being a bitch to Cliff."

Bill frowned. "Dragon?" He shook his head. "That's all that happened?"

"No, I suppose not." I glanced behind me at Blue. "She did try to get me to sign a restraining order against all of the Carlsons."

"She had a restraining order with her?" Bill asked. His raised eyebrows created deep furrows in his ample forehead.

"Civilians may request and receive blank legal documents,"

Blue said.

"What of it? I asked you to keep your trap shut, Kendall."

"I am sorry, sir. The suspect appeared to be trying to incriminate her victim with her testimony."

His low, musical voice nearly drew me from my seat in rage. I wanted nothing more to get in Blue's face, teeth gnashing, and ask him just what the hell his problem was, and how often Marguerite let him share her bed in exchange for tormenting me.

But of course that was exactly what he wanted me to do. Losing my temper right in front of Bill would give him leave to say, *See? This girl is a menace, no matter how many hands of bridge you play with her pop.*

I held my tongue. Bill removed the problem for me. "Dwight D, why don't you and Kendall take a cup of coffee outside, please?

"Yes, sir." Dwight D laid a massive paw on Blue's back and ushered him out the door.

Bill sighed. "I appreciate your honesty, Bethany. Since you admit to being at her house, and to a heated conversation, I'll have to write up a domestic disturbance report. Since you are lawful family of Marguerite, it will just look like a spat that went too far.

"And I apologize for Kendall. He has a tremendous record, believe it or not. He just hasn't gotten the hang of Auburn yet. He'll either come around in a month or two, or leave." He shrugged and rubbed his palm over the remaining strands of hair combed over his pate as if to say, *Either way.*

He touched me, came to my lips, but I buried it. Violation or not, Blue technically had done nothing wrong. His frisking had been quick and business-like, no matter how wrong it had felt.

"You can sit with Dwight D while he files the report, and then you can go home," he said. "And for what it's worth, I'm sorry."

17

I spent the next day packing for my trip back out to Maine. A week of work at the museum on Dad's generous payroll had paid for my airline ticket. Initially he'd wanted to join me, but I wasn't sure how long I would be gone, and Dad hated leaving the museum for more than a day or two.

"I'll call every couple days if it makes you feel better," I told him.

"At least call to tell me what kind of car you rent," he said. The crow's feet at the corners of his eyes crinkled up with amusement.

By afternoon I was packed. Like I had everyday since coming home, I checked the mail for a letter from Cliff. I didn't know if mental hospitals allowed patients to send letters to friends or family, but I couldn't figure out any reason they wouldn't. After a week, though, I had lost hope of hearing from him. Again, if he thought I had walked out on him, why would he write? I would have written myself if I thought Eleanor would not see my letters.

Today there was a manila packaging envelope mixed in with the rest of the letters. No return address, but the postal mark read *Bangor, ME* and bore the urgent red and blue eagle sticker of Priority Mail. My name and address were in Cliff's clear, tidy handwriting.

I rushed inside, dumped the other mail on the kitchen island and fled to my room. Inside there was no letter or even a note from Cliff, except for a folded piece of yellow legal paper with an address written on it:

Motel 6
1100 Hammond St.
Bangor, ME 04401

I stuffed the paper into the side pocket of my duffel bag and dumped the package's only other contents on my bed: a CD in a jewel case.

The words "Bethany's Mix" had been written with a blue grease pencil in strange handwriting that was somehow both loopy and jagged.

I opened the jewel case and took out the disc with shaking hands. Even though the CD had obviously been burned on a computer, my stereo read it just fine.

The first sounds on the disc were rough and scratchy, as if someone were rubbing coarse fabric across a microphone. Then I heard the voices, distant and dull, but still audible:

"Eeesskiffta," a child's voice said.

"No, Clifford." Eleanor's prissy, nasal voice, but higher in pitch. "Heath...cliff...ton. Just try the first one again. Heath," she enunciated.

"Heeesss."

"Hey, you got the 'H' this time. Good job."

The recording clicked loudly, making me jump.

"Now try it all together." Eleanor's voice again. The ambient noise in the recording had changed slightly. I wondered if this section had been recorded on a different day than the first part.

"Heathcliffta Marbob Cawssonippy."

I laughed aloud, even as the tears began to flow. The voice was so darn *cute*. But the significance of what I was hearing was apparent: Cliff was learning the only words he would ever be able to control. And Eleanor was at the helm.

The CD played for nearly eighty minutes, telling a skillful story in familiar voices. I listened to the bulk of it curled up on my bed, alternately hugging my pillow and whapping it against my headboard when I heard something especially shocking.

I must have murmured, "How did she do this?" twenty times in less than an hour-and-a-half. And before the disc had delivered its final heartbreaking message, I had cursed myself twice that many times for ever leaving Maine.

But how could I have known?

When the digital readout on my stereo read 79:32, Cliff's voice came on one final time, only it wasn't from years ago. This was the clear tenor voice which had assured me, "Nice to meet you, Victor Hugo," when I had asked him if he wanted to go out for ice cream one evening this past June. This was the voice of my husband.

"I love you, Bethany," it said. "Please come back."

Part 4:

Eleanor

1

I had never been called a cunt before.

"Seventeen-year-olds don't need permission to get married in Michigan, you dumb cunt."

Rewind.

"...get married in Michigan, you dumb cunt."

Rewind.

"...ichigan, you dumb cunt."

That cold voice, over and over in my headphones as I stared at myself in the hotel's bathroom mirror. It was awful.

And undeserved, I thought. After all, I hadn't *asked* them to drive that old limousine. And I certainly hadn't asked Morticia Addams to marry Clifford and drown herself in the cesspool that is the Carlson family.

But when she called me that word—that filthy nasty word worse than anything I'd ever been called by Mother or KB or even by people at school when they think I'm too far away to hear—something else occurred to me: I had never asked to hunt down Clifford, either. I just hadn't refused.

2

"Eleanor, do you like your nose?"

What kind of question was that? Mother knew perfectly well how much I hated my nose—how I strained my eyes trying to watch my profile in the bathroom mirror at night, and trying to see someone besides the Wicked Witch of the West. I was sure she was baiting me (it hadn't even been twenty-four hours since I'd whacked her with the spatula and Mother's grudges didn't fade like the red mark on her cheek had done), but to what end? She didn't usually pick fights when KB was over, and I could see his booted feet crossed on Aunt Alice's coffee table from my spot in front of the kitchen sink.

I cursed myself for not switching the tape in the recorder under the couch KB now lounged on. (It would have run out at 2:00 this afternoon, I knew, having picked up nothing more interesting than Mother periodically stalking through the living room in perfect time with Aunt Alice's mantle clock. She had no idea she did this but the tapes never lie.) If I had changed the tape I would have heard what the two of them had been debating since supper. At least, their tone *suggested* debate—none of their words had carried over the racket I made clumsily washing dishes with a plastic bag rubber banded over my new cast to keep it dry.

And now she brought up my nose. I know a stage prompt when I hear one; this idiotic question meant the curtain was about to go up in the living room and I needed to be front-and-center when it did. *I like my nose just fine,* the reply popped into my head as I peeled the wet plastic bag off my cast. *This* schnoz *can smell the shit on KB's boots all the way out here.* I bit my bottom lip to keep any of it from tumbling out. I was still on probation from last night. I ran a sweaty hand over my new cast.

KB, still in his uniform, had one arm slung lazily around Mother's shoulders, as I knew he would. He had moved the coffee table closer to the couch so his short legs could reach it. His dark eyes flicked up and down my body—again, as I knew they would—and registered their familiar disgust before returning hungrily to my mother. I had decided long ago I would scream if anyone ever looked at me like he looked at Mother; I could almost see the greasy streaks his gaze left on her cleavage and bare thighs.

Not that I could blame him; Mother's hair was up in a fiery ponytail and her yellow spaghetti-strap top made her summer tan the color of a polished penny. Even having seen her up close every day of my life, her beauty still made me want to shiver. To have a *tenth* of that...

He whispered something in her ear and chuckled deeply as I came into the room. She hushed him primly, although she seemed on the verge of laughter as well. For a moment they looked like the couples I watched at school: both trying to make an unfunny joke funny, but appear too cool to be amused at the same time.

I hated KB.

"So?" she prompted.

She could not make me talk about my appearance in front of him. I would stand here and take whatever they wanted to give, but I would do it with sealed lips.

I doubted I would like what either of them said in the next few minutes, but I undid the second button on my jacket and tugged the lapel—and the new cylindrical digital recorder in my breast pocket ("Extra Small—No Tapes Needed!")—out toward them as much as I could without being too obvious. No matter what they said, good or bad, I knew I would listen to it again before I went to sleep. Maybe even burn the conversation to CD if it was interesting enough. The last one of those had come from the machine under Mother's nightstand, with the two of them trying to decide how I would address KB. He wanted me to call him "Officer Blue" and Mother said if he was going to frequent our house, I should call him "Kendall." In the end they decided on his initials, which was, according to their recorded conversations, hip enough to be friendly, but with more respectful distance than being on a mutual first-name basis. His indignant splutter when Mother had said I should call him by his first name had been way too hilarious simply to erase the tape as I normally did. Not only that, Mother had defended me. That alone was worth the price of a blank CD. The noises that followed I edited out. (I had also considered burning the recording from inside my jacket to CD last night, but one time hearing that wet slap when the spatula connected with Mother's face was plenty. Not to mention that bony jingle of Mother dangling Cliff's car keys out toward him right before he ran. I jammed the erase button on the digital recorder after only a second or two of that noise.)

Mother saw I wouldn't play ball tonight and cut to the chase—literally, it turned out. "You have asked me to pay for a nose job. You have asked to go to a dermatologist for your acne. You even mentioned your high hairline at one point, didn't you?"

My face burned. KB smirked. Despite my jacket and capris, I felt like I was standing stark naked in front of them.

Mother stood and moved between KB and me. His smirk disappeared as soon as he didn't have her to hang onto.

Then her face was all I saw, beautiful and bronzed from the same sunshine that was killing her sister. Her green eyes caught mine and held them. As always, I found I just wanted to stare at those eyes for as long as I could—to study the flashing golden flecks that made them seem to glow in the right lighting. Eyes that made me want to cry because I would never have them, and, even worse, because I would never see the warmth I wanted to see in them.

"My answer is yes."

KB was gone. The living room was gone. Mother was all that mattered. "What do you mean?" Later that night, listening to this exchange again, I was surprised to hear I had whispered.

"If you can find your cousin and bring him back to me, I will give you all those things. I will make you beautiful."

Ten years ago, if Mother had hinted that I was not, in fact, beautiful, I would have been crushed. By this point, though, I was quite used to the idea.

That same whisper piped through my headphones as I lay in bed, forcefully reminding me of the earliest recordings of my voice, when I had still played with a red-headed Barbie doll and her beautiful baby Kelly. "Okay."

3

Can't sleep?

The note glowed up from Clifford's new Palm Pilot in the semi-darkness of our room. His curious, concerned eyes shone in the canned light seeping through the curtains from the motel sign outside the window. The large Band-Aids on his forehead and cheek seemed to glisten in that light.

"Bad voices," I said, tapping the side of my head with an index finger. I had coined this excuse when Clifford and I were six. He had beaten me at checkers for the first time ever, and he had known it wasn't because of any new strategy on his part. The night before, Mother had stuck her head in the bathroom while I sang "Papa Don't Preach" in the shower and laughingly asked if I was strangling a cat in there. My very first recorder (at the time, my *only* recorder) had been running in my jean jacket on the floor by my towel, and caught both my singing and the subsequent comment. All through my game with Cliff, my mind had played the broken record: *"Papa dun PREACH! Ummee lumamee. Papa DUN preach!"* I hadn't even known the words. The worst part was, in my bed that night, under the increasingly familiar yoke of headphones, I *had* sounded like a cat. Not being strangled, necessarily; maybe in a fight, maybe broadcasting its loud desire for a mate. But I had assumed until then that I had a lovely singing voice, and especially enjoyed the resonant buzz that began in my nose and vibrated through my whole head when I sang.

"Papa Don't Preach" was the end of that dream. And the beginning of "bad voices." Clifford had taken what I said at face value then. Ever since, it seemed that as far as he was concerned, those two words would satisfactorily explain even my foulest mood.

Now, Clifford nodded at this, set the Palm Pilot almost reverently in its charging dock and, rolled over. In the dim, yet somehow harsh light from the Palm Pilot, I saw his chest hitch a couple times as he settled the blankets around him—the bruise on his left arm, just below the shoulder, was an ugly purple, and still spreading. I wondered how he kept from screaming every time he rolled over in his sleep. I doubted my arm had ever hurt as bad as his did right now. His breathing evened out in a minute or two.

I fluffed my pillow vigorously and tried to follow his example. I was certainly tired enough to sleep.

So why couldn't I?

The "bad voices"? I had been hearing them since the first night I plugged my first pair of headphones into my first recorder at six years old, to rediscover the sounds of the day. Still, there had never been so many voices as there had been in the last two weeks. Nor had they ever been this loud.

One solution was obvious: tell someone else what the voices were saying. Divide their volume in half. Clifford was right over there, in the room's other bed. And who better to share one's darkest secrets than someone who couldn't repeat them?

I fell asleep thinking what a great idea that was.

4

Sometimes things look different in the morning. I found that, without the darkness to stew in, I wasn't nearly as eager to tell Clifford *anything* about my bad voices. Especially that they were literal voices, rather than some vague metaphor I had kept up for twelve years. That was a secret I might keep to myself for a good long time yet, in fact; I had an idea that people would be much less likely to say interesting things if they knew a digital recorder was industriously immortalizing every word they said, and I wasn't ready to give up the small silver tube in my breast pocket just yet.

Clifford was already awake, sitting up with his bottom half still under covers, fiddling with his Palm Pilot. He looked five again, taking seemingly random pokes at the screen with the stylus, tragic spikes of hair leaping from his scalp, above the bandages, in every direction like lemmings dipped in orange Kool-Aid.

"You hungry?"

"I love being a turtle," he said, nodding. He didn't look up from the Palm Pilot. *Boys and their toys,* I thought.

Well, maybe *Carlsons* and their toys. Hadn't I hunched on

my bed for over an hour the night I bought my digital recorder, almost feverish to learn every trick and feature the bug had to offer?

Watching Clifford poke and jab intently with the stylus brought on a fresh surge of the alien fondness I had been feeling for him in the day and a half since I quite literally tore his wife away from him. And with it, the familiar throb of terror that my mother would find out I had disobeyed her. Or worse, that she might know right now that Clifford was not in a hospital (even though I had taken great pains to give that impression to her), and we were killing time in a motel on her dime. Oh, and she would be so frosted to see Clifford stabbing at the five-hundred-dollar toy that was now on her credit card; she had launched into a fabulous conniption two years ago when Alice bought Clifford his crappy little car, and it hadn't cost her a cent.

I hugged my arms to my stomach, all too aware of the scratchy fiberglass cast weighing down my left arm. Life could become very unpleasant if Mother found out about all this.

"I'm going to McDonald's before I start hearing those damn chains again, and worry away my appetite," I said, and almost clapped my hand over my mouth in shock.

Now Clifford did turn away from his toy, frowning. I'd read in novels that people sometimes "burst into tears," but I hadn't thought it was possible until now; the concern in his green eyes seemed to tap a well of emotion so deep and powerful that I thought tears might just explode from my eyes. I leapt for the door, simultaneously praying that Clifford had not seen how close I had come to losing it right in front of him, knowing he *had* seen, and feeling somehow glad for it.

"Two breakfast burritos?" I asked on my way out the door. I could hardly believe that high, watery shriek had come from me.

"There's a hole in my bucket," he said. I knew without turning around that he meant yes.

♪

I had hoped to outrun the dread I felt while cradling my cast back in the room. Either McDonald's wasn't far enough away, or Clifford's Toyota wasn't fast enough. But here it was—in Bangor, Maine, waiting at a stoplight—fight or flight, and it seemed I couldn't flee. One more battle, then, in a long series of them. Always in a car, it seemed, always when I was alone. My life for the past week and a half, in other words.

Fine, I thought. Let the memories come for yet another rematch.

They did.

It was the first and only time Mother was not beautiful. I suppose I was no prize myself, standing in the kitchen with a kitchen knife to my arm, but I was upset. Neither Mother nor Clifford had mentioned the napkins I folded. And then that rubbish about toasting buns? Last time I'd made hot dogs and toasted the buns, Mother had complained throughout dinner that they tasted like she was licking the inside of a charcoal grill.

Anyway, Clifford knew I would never really cut myself. That part was just a joke.

But the keys were not a joke—Mother holding up the keys to Clifford's car while he was on the verge of taking off anyway. The next night, fumbling around my new cast, I dumped the previous day's contents from my digital recorder onto my laptop's hard drive and created a continuous loop of the keys' jingling. The sound was smaller than I thought it should be. I added weight and reverberation with my sound-editing software until they sounded as heavy on the recording as they did in my memory. In the dark, as I lay in bed, I listened to the three seconds of jingling over and over for maybe a half-hour. I don't remember turning up the volume, but by the time I tore off my headphones and tossed them across my room, the sound was deafening. Even lying ten feet away on the floor, the jingling seemed to grow to fill the whole room like the chains of Marley's ghost.

Which, of course, is the simile that had me holed up in a Motel 6 with my idiot cousin in a strange, humid part of the country where mosquitoes the size of hummingbirds lumbered nightly into the sky and hung on our window with bloated bodies like cherry tomatoes. The mosquitoes added yet another unpleasant image to that night: Mother's mouth had seemed too red as she leered at Clifford, jingling his keys at him. I could easily imagine her popping a couple of those mosquitoes for lipstick—one good squeeze for upper and lower lips.

Mrs. Marley and her mosquitoes, I thought now, navigating Clifford's car through unfamiliar streets. I laughed aloud, even though the thought wasn't funny. I laughed to escape the fear that underneath Mother's perfect skin there was something terrible happening. I laughed to escape the new uncertainty I'd had about her since that night; it's awful to wonder if there is something unkind within your own mother. I kept telling myself there could not be, but wasn't I disobeying her right now because of that uncertainty?

No, I realized. I was not disobeying out of uncertainty. If not for the last memory of that night which came back to blacken my mind's eye, as it always did, I would *only* be uncertain, and

Clifford would be in the hospital Mother thought he was in. KB had only missed Clifford's exit by a minute or two. During that interminable time, Mother and I had faced off in the kitchen. I still bore the knife, Mother the keys, but this was not a physical match. Our eyes were locked, each of us unable to believe what the other had just done, each of us daring the other to admit her wrong.

KB strode into this scene through the back door like he was part of the family. I don't know if Mother invited him over for the evening, or if he just popped in for some fellowship and a hot dog with an untoasted bun. Either way, he saw me with a knife, and his girlfriend unarmed. Without a sound, he leapt to my side, grabbed my wrist in one small, powerful hand, and squeezed. There was a crack and the knife hit the floor. Hot pain lanced up my arm like an injection of boiling water. Still he held my wrist.

"Are you okay?" he asked Mother.

The hand holding Clifford's keys dropped to her side, and the other came up to rub her face again where I had struck her with the spatula. "Pick up the knife, Eleanor," she said.

"Mother, my wrist really—"

"Once you clean up you may eat supper." Her voice was distant and soft, as if she were daydreaming about running through an open field.

KB stepped fluidly in front of me, twisting my wrist slightly as he did so. I wanted to cry out, and I almost did, but I didn't want KB to know he could hurt me any more than he had. I straightened up and met his eyes defiantly. I wish I hadn't; even though he was in street clothes, he had a leather case for handcuffs on his belt, and he pulled them out now. He clamped them first onto my healthy wrist, then the hurt one. At the time, I thought I had managed to keep from making any noise, but the recording from my jacket pocket revealed a high, slow moan when he closed the second cuff. He winked.

When he turned to Mother, I held up my shackles to her in a silent plea. She was upset with me, and for good cause, but she was my mother. Next thing KB knew, he would be in the back yard with a bruised ass from being kicked out the door.

She didn't even look at me. KB led her gently from the kitchen, murmuring greasy comforts.

Twenty minutes later the skin on either side of the left cuff was an angry red, and swollen to the point where the silver cuff had almost disappeared. I refused to show KB what he had done to me, but Mother must have heard me crying. "Let me see," she said, and I began crying even harder at the care in her voice. I hadn't even heard her come into the kitchen.

She gasped. *"Kendall!"*

That's right, I celebrated behind tightly squeezed eyelids. *No care in her voice for you, KB. JUST ME!*

Then KB's heavy boots thumped their way into the kitchen. "What'd she do, stick her hands in hot water? How dumb can—"

When my mother gets into one of her moods, people around her lose the ability to finish their sentences. "You will get your fucking traps off my daughter's hands this instant, and if even one more tear rolls down her cheek while you do it, you will never set foot in this house again."

After Mother banished the sulky KB, she sat with me in my room all night, periodically refilling the sandwich bag of ice on my wrist and brewing cup after cup of Sleepytime Tea to calm me until the swelling had gone down enough to take me to the hospital for a cast.

6

When I got back to the motel, cold burritos in hand (I had driven around the block several times in an attempt to get my emotions back under control—I exhausted the entire box of Kleenex Clifford always kept in his car in the three blocks between the hotel and McDonalds), the Palm Pilot was back in its charging dock and the TV was on. I tossed him the burritos. He gave me the thumbs-up and tore into the first one.

"How is it?" I asked. Part of me wanted him to spit it back out in disgust and complain (in a series of involved gestures, of course) that the burritos were too cold to eat, and what kind of cousin was I to cap off these two days of betrayal with a cold three-dollar breakfast? And with no coffee or juice to wash it down? Jeez-Louise, Eleanor, how can anyone suck as bad as you?

Instead, the thumbs came up again and he downed the rest of the burrito with his second bite. As if to insult me further, he rubbed his belly and offered some unintelligible praise around a mouthful of tortilla and eggs.

I flopped down on my bed, knowing full well how unreasonable I was to be angry with him for appreciating me, but unable to do anything about it. "What is this crap you're watching?" I said.

More noise escaped Clifford's clogged mouth. I wondered why he even bothered answering people's questions sometimes.

On the screen, two very ugly people—one short and fat, the other tall and skinny—were bebopping down a filthy city street wearing black suits with black ties, black fedoras, and black sunglasses. I was determined to hold onto my foul mood as long as possible, but suddenly I couldn't. The two ugly men kept repeating this nonsensical line throughout the rest of the movie that didn't sound nonsensical to me at all. The point of their adventure was apparently to show people singing and dancing in different parts of the dirty city, but every time another character stopped singing or dancing long enough to ask these ugly men what they were about, one or both of them would answer, "We're on a mission from God." But they spoke with phony accents so thick that "God" sounded like "Gaad." Typically, I found myself unable to control either my emotions or my body movements as I watched the movie, and each time this ridiculous line came out, "We're on a mission from Gaad," I felt a huge stone splash into my belly, and I nodded like a marionette.

Near the end of the movie an actress I recognized as having been Princess Leia in the Star Wars movies, and who had been chasing the tall man and short man (*The Blues Brothers*, Clifford clarified on his Palm Pilot), faced them down in a sewer tunnel with a machine gun. Then she called the fat one a "contemptible pig" and a "miserable slug." She said other stuff too, but I quit listening; the words coming from her mouth had to be very ugly indeed for her to spit them out that way. I had thought the Blues Brothers were unpleasant when I first saw them, but they were beauty queens compared to Princess Leia in this scene. Even when she wasn't talking, it was a toss-up whether she showed more eyes or teeth. I almost expected her to reach behind her back, pull out the keys to the Blues Brothers' beat up police car, and jingle them menacingly in their faces.

"She's a monster!" I yelled. It was a harsh sound in the small room.

Clifford jumped and stared at me, wide-eyed. I didn't care.

"What did they ever do to her?" I said. He nodded carefully, as if he were just trying to soothe me, which I'm sure he was. I'm sure he was just as mystified by my sudden ire as I was.

"I'm going to call Mother," I said, sliding off the bed. "You shouldn't watch things like this, Clifford."

"I'm going to need you to stay where you are for a few days, honey."

I yanked my cell phone away from my ear as if it had come alive and bitten my ear.

"Eleanor? Did you hear me?"

"Yes, Mother. I'm sorry." I couldn't let it go. "You said once Cliff was in the hospital I could come back home.

Her voice hardened. "I don't need you to remind me what I said. Now I'm saying something else. If you want to be angry with someone, you can be angry at Cliff's trollop for not staying gone. Who knows what he told her before you caught up with them." So now I had been too slow. The message was as clear as if she had said it aloud. She went on in a softer tone: "Besides, she might be upset enough to hurt you if you come back, and I could never forgive myself if that happened."

Well, Bethany *had* seemed awfully pissed off when she left the hospital. But if there had ever been a time to take a swing at me, it was right after I'd torn up their marriage license. I still hadn't shared that little chestnut.

"Did you make an appointment with the surgeon?" I heard (and hated) the pleading desperation in my voice.

"We'll do it first thing when you get home. How is Cliff liking his new home?" I wasn't sure if there had been more suppressed laughter in the first or second sentence.

"He likes it just fine," I said. "Everyone's very nice to him, and he gets all the paper he wants to write notes and draw pictures for the other patients."

"I see." Breathing. "Maybe I'll call this hospital and remind them my dear nephew is dangerous, and he's not there for a vacation."

"*I'll* do it!" I said, and pounded my cast against my thigh. When would I learn not to bait Mother? "There's one big fat nurse who doesn't like Clifford at all. Says his head looks like a cactus someone beat with a golf club. I could request that she take care of him most days."

More breathing. She was trying to hear the lie, but, as usual, offering specifics made her less suspicious. "That will be fine. As long as they remember their hospital is not a resort."

There was something petulant and childish in that last comment. Suddenly I was furious. "I'll talk to Nurse Sanchez. The fat one. Goodbye, Mother."

7

The tunnel smells of sulfur and piss. I hear footfalls splashing toward me, two silhouettes appear around a bend ahead. They keep looking behind them, and as their heads turn, I see they are both wearing fedoras like Indiana Jones. Or the Blues Brothers. *They obviously don't know I'm here.*

My left hand carries a familiar weight—I realize the weight is not my cast, but a gun. A machine gun, I am not surprised to see. Without thinking, I level the gun at the two approaching silhouettes. They can't be more than ten feet away now.

The shorter one sees me first, and holds out an arm to stop the tall one. They step cautiously forward until I can see their faces in the gloom. I am once again unsurprised to see Clifford and Bethany. The latter's lipstick is even blacker than her hat and suit. She whips a paper from the breast pocket of her black suit. The paper is shaped like a small knight's shield and glows faintly. "We're on a mission from God!" she bellows, and I quake at the power in her voice.

Whether out of fear or some other internal directive, I squeeze the trigger and the gun roars its thunder through the tunnel. The muzzle flashes create a vivid picture show in which the shield Bethany holds up gets blown apart like toilet paper in a hurricane.

I fire until all my ammunition is spent, but Clifford and Bethany are still standing. The empty shell casings lay in the muck around my feet and begin to bubble. When the first bubble pops, a heavy, putrid mosquito brrrrr's into the air with a sound like a B-17 bomber.

Bethany shrieks. She grabs Clifford's hand, and they run past me, bowling me over into the stew coursing through the tunnel.

More bubbles pop now—the tunnel floor is practically boiling—and each releases another brrrrr-ing mosquito. They have to be big, I see now; they all carry a long chain of keys below them.

The first mosquito drops its payload onto my shoulder. Free of this weight, it alights on my forehead and begins drinking noisily through a proboscis the size of a toothpick. I brush off the first string of keys, and slap the first mosquito, which sprays my own blood all over my face and into my eyes. Now that I can't see to fight them off, all the mosquitoes attack at once, first dropping their keys, then setting down to feed. In seconds the combined weight of the keys and bloated mosquitoes pulls me deeper into the muck. I feel it creep up my neck, into my ears, then eagerly around my mouth and into my eyes like groping fingers.

From somewhere outside my body, I watch my long nose go under last, like the mast of a sinking ship.

8

A lifetime of wearing an extra layer of denim over my regular clothes in all seasons has made me a cold sleeper. I am used to sleeping under a down comforter throughout the year. I woke from that dream with my face buried in a pillow—truly suffocating—and lying in a wet spot the size of my entire body. The moisture and my inability to breath brought on a fresh wave of panic. Even after I realized I had just sweated through the sheets and was not drowning in a puddle of scum at the bottom of a sewer pipe, I still couldn't sleep.

I stripped off my nightclothes and hung them on the towel rack in the bathroom to dry. My denim jacket was folded on the counter, digital recorder inside. This was in my hand, recording my voice before I realized I had either picked it up or intended to speak.

"My name is Eleanor Roberta Carlson," the freckled, ghostly-pale nude girl in the mirror told me and the recorder. "And *I* am on a mission from God."

9

After my dream I puttered around the room and lay wakefully in bed until about six. By then I was so pissed from insomnia, I decided to get out of the room for awhile. I had seen a Dunkin Donuts on the way to McDonalds yesterday. Maybe Clifford would like a chocolate long john and coffee when he woke up.

Most of the mosquitoes were already asleep, or wherever they went during the day; only one hung lazily from the outside of our window. I thought about smacking it, but remembered too clearly the gout of blood and rotten wetness I'd felt as I'd crushed the mosquito in my dream, like squishing an old tomato, and I left it alone.

Once I was in the car, driving with the windows down, I was glad I'd gotten up. Early morning turned out to be the most pleasant time of day in this soggy marsh of a state. Straight rows of high clouds caught the rising sun's light and cast a lovely orange light over the waking city. Many cars were already on the road, but no one tailgated, or honked his horn, or revved his engine through a yellow light. Perhaps everyone was simply too groggy from the weekend to carry out the usual indecencies of city driving, but there was a new peace in this calm rush of humanity that previously I had only found under my headphones. By the time I pulled into Dunkin Donuts I was humming with a song on the radio that I didn't even know.

Clifford killed my mood when I got back. He was outside our room, pulling the door shut, as I drove in. He only had on his pajama bottoms. Even in the orange morning light, his face was dead white and he looked terrified, as if his fear wouldn't let the sun warm him. When he saw the car, he slumped to the sidewalk and leaned back against the door with his arms around his knees.

Who died? I almost yelled when I got out of the car. I realized that wouldn't be very sensitive and held my tongue. But I was still annoyed with him for getting my heart rate back up after such a relaxing drive. I settled for, "What's the matter with you?" I regretted how unkind I sounded, which annoyed me even more.

He looked around dumbly, then picked up a small white rock. He scratched into the sidewalk, *Thought u left.*

It wasn't until then that I realized how often Clifford had been "left" by people close to him recently. First his mother, then his wife (*MY FAULT!* my mind shrieked. *First I made him leave at the worst time, then I made* her *leave at the worst time. MY FAULT!*), and now he thought I had left too. In addition to horrid guilt, this chain of thoughts led me to another realization: he was worried I had left. He *wanted* me around.

I had kneeled beside him, but I stood abruptly. The motel, the parking lot, Clifford—all of it vanished. I saw myself in the bathroom mirror, stark naked and vulnerable, but strong. *I am on a mission from God*, I'd said. Suddenly I knew what that mission was.

When I looked back down at Clifford he was staring at me with a species of wonder. No one had ever looked at me that way. It made me feel stronger and uncomfortable at the same time. "I bought us breakfast," I said. "And we'll need it. We have work to do."

The last time I'd tried this I'd had no time limit and no motive except my own curiosity. I still didn't know how long I had, but I guessed Mother would want me home in less than a week. She was setting up Aunt Alice's funeral, after all, and I would need to be there for that even if she didn't want Clifford there (and I thought she might want him there in the end; she knew he needed a chance to say goodbye even more than the rest of us).

But before any of that would happen I had to get Bethany back here. Mother had said she was already in Auburn again. That seemed awfully fast; until I talked to Mother, I had expected to wake up every morning to Bethany's angry pounding on the motel door.

Her leaving so quickly meant she was even more upset than she had seemed in the hospital—

(Seventeen-year-olds don't need permission to get married in Michigan, you dumb cunt)

—and she had seemed pretty angry. What worried me was that if she was just angry at me, she probably would have been pounding on our door two days ago. But maybe she was angry at *Clifford* for leaving too, or for allowing me to take him away. Maybe she had come to the conclusion that Clifford didn't love her enough to stay around. I had thought the same thing myself until I sneaked a peak at what Clifford had been doing on his Palm Pilot over the weekend. All his random poking with the stylus hadn't been random at all; in the middle of the night, waiting for my dream to fade and the sun to come up, I had turned on his new toy and found several pages of letters to Bethany. They weren't desperate or mushy, he just related what we were doing, that I had bought him breakfast once already and was being an all-around pal, like he and I were at some bizarre type of Motel 6 summer camp, and our week would be up soon.

At the end of all this, he had written, "I love you. See you soon. Cliff."

Well, even if Clifford didn't realize how serious my mother

was about putting him away forever and ever, I did. If we went back home to reunite him with Bethany, he might last fifteen minutes in Auburn before being tossed on the next bus to Terra Haute. So the only option left was to bring her up here again.

"Clifford," I said, opening the door to our room an ushering him in, "we're going to get your wife back."

He nodded.

"We're going to have to work much faster this time. But I'm not worried. We've done it before."

He sat down on his bed, took my hands in his own, and brought them up to his cheeks. A bonfire danced behind his eyes.

I contorted his mouth into the appropriate shape with my hands, taking care not to let my cast brush the sore spots on his face. "Make a sound," I commanded.

10

Thursday night we had it. What had taken a month when we were six, we accomplished in less than four days. I made him speak into my iBook (I still wasn't ready for him to know about the recorder in my jacket) and afterward we went out to Quiznos to celebrate. It was at Quiznos where the planets fell out of alignment. Pick any overused metaphor you like: my bubble of false serenity popped; the floor fell out from under my feet; my world came crashing to a halt; whatever.

It was bad.

I had finished about a quarter of my sandwich. Clifford was nearly done with his, and eyeing the rest of mine. He almost looked like himself a week out of the hospital—he still wore two Band-Aids over the worst road rash on his cheek and forehead, and a faint streak of yellow and green under his right eye was the last reminder of what had been a wicked shiner. And he could certainly pack away the food, cracked ribs or not.

Then my cell phone vibrated at my hip. I must have jumped a foot out of my seat. Clifford nearly shot lettuce out of his nose at my reaction. I scowled. "It's not funny, Clifford. Now shut up or Mother will hear you." I opened the phone. "Hello,

Mother."

"What's the matter?"

"The phone startled me." I hated her daily calls. At first her suspicion had kept me awake at night, wondering if she knew how flamboyantly I was disobeying her. But I realized it was much simpler than that: she was suspicious that, each day, I had screwed something up. Anything.

"You didn't talk to the pharmacy, did you?"

The other night it was, "You didn't talk to Nurse Sanchez, did you?" While I was on the road it had been, "You didn't let them get too far ahead, did you?"

Yesterday she had told me to make sure the hospital wasn't giving Clifford so many drugs that he didn't know where he was. "He needs to know where he is and who put him there," she'd said. Even without my recorder, I remembered her exact words.

"Believe me, he knows exactly where he is and who 'put him there,'" I'd told her, aping her tone. This had been met with that eyes-narrowed silence she was so good at on the phone—the silence that made me want to confess every lie I'd ever told, every bad thing I'd ever done, just to get her to say something.

"Of course I talked to the pharmacy," I told her now. "When in the last week have I not done something you asked me to do?" *Besides* every *time*, I thought, and turned the cell away from my mouth in case I couldn't suppress all of my sudden giggles.

The silence was briefer tonight. Then the conversation turned south. "Alice's memorial service is on Monday," she said.

"On my birthday?" I said. Cliff glanced up from the last bit of his sandwich. My stomach gurgled restlessly. "On *Clifford's* birthday?" I whispered.

Silence.

"Mother, don't you think that's a little—" *tasteless*, I wanted to say, but curbed my tongue: "too much?"

"Too much," she repeated, her voice now dangerously quiet, like it was whenever I expressed an idea too adult for her liking.

"Too much for *me*," I backpedaled. "I don't want to come

home and have a funeral first thing, then my birthday party. It doesn't seem right."

Her laughter pealed through the phone like notes on a xylophone. "Honey, I need you up there. How would it look if we left Cliff alone in a mental hospital on the day of his own mother's memorial service? Don't worry, though, I'll tell everyone you're with him, keeping him company as we remember Alice. You'll be a real hero," she said dryly.

The plastic cell phone creaked in my grip. Clifford watched me closely now, his last bite of sandwich forgotten on the table. The subtext was unmistakable, as it always was with Mother. My script for Monday—which Mother assumed I would deliver in Clifford's white padded room—would be along the lines of: *Happy birthday! You're missing your mom's funeral! And, by the way, you'll never leave Maine again, or even this hospital. Nor will you see your wife again—she might even be in jail by now. Silly you for thinking you could just leave and be happy.*

Suddenly I felt something cold and very hard on the back of my head. The tile floor, I realized. Clifford was standing over me. Along with three strangers wearing Quiznos shirts. One of them held Clifford's Palm Pilot, reading whatever Clifford had written on the screen. A second one asked, "Are you alright, Miss?"

I cleared my throat. "I'm on a mission from God." Out of the corner of my eye I saw an overturned chair. Clifford reached out a hand and I let him pull me into a sitting position. Embarrassment began to creep in, like an icy breeze through my jean jacket. Goosebumps rose on my arms, even under my cast.

"My niece has epilepsy," the second Quiznos worker told me helpfully.

"Yeah, my great uncle had it too," said the one who still had Clifford's Palm Pilot.

The third one piped up for the first time. "Don't worry about your phone. We'll clean up the mess, and I'm sure your company can send you a new one. They're pretty good about that."

Clifford recovered his toy from the apparent leader of these morons, and patted him on the arm. He subtly aimed the screen at me as he helped me to my feet: *This is my cousin Eleanor. She had an epileptic seizure, but she will be fine. Sorry about the commotion, and thanks for understanding.* Which still wouldn't have explained why he couldn't *tell* them this, but maybe this had been his second note.

"Can we get out of here?" I said. My cheeks burned, and two of the Quiznos guys were staring at me in open wonder.

Clifford put his arm around me and steered me toward the door. I heard a strange tinkling sound and saw where the third guy had gone. A scattered pile of silvery debris glittered across about three feet of the floor against the far wall. He had retrieved a broom to sweep it up.

"Is that my phone?"

11

The CD with Clifford's second purposeful speech in over a decade lay in its jewel case on the nightstand, ready to be shipped off to Auburn. I blinked the morning gum from my eyes. Beyond the CD, Clifford had left his Palm Pilot turned toward me with a message: *Getting breakfast. Back soon.*

I sat up and reached for the ceiling, relishing the pops in my shoulder and back. My jacket was still on. And my capris. The comforter showed a narrow indentation where I had slept, and a sweat puddle the size of Lake Erie darkened my pillow, but otherwise the bed was still made.

Random images started clicking on in my head, like a vivid slideshow: Mother's phone call; the tinkling of my shattered cell phone as Quiznos guy pushed his broom; handing Clifford the keys to his own car like a designated driver...

And that was it. I must have fallen asleep on the way home. Clifford must have *carried* me from the car to bed so gently that I never even woke up.

A plastic key card rattled the door. Clifford strode in proudly, bearing a paper sack of donuts. He pitched me a carton of Tropicana orange juice.

"I'm so stupid."

He froze with his hand in the sack.

"Who was I to think *I* could ever be on a mission from God?" I sobbed. "It's *you*, Clifford. You're always the one. So much bad stuff has happened to you, and you're still nice and wonderful." I drew in a wet breath around what felt like gallons of snot and tears. "*I'm hideous!*" I shrieked.

Clifford pitched the donut sack onto the counter by the TV and picked up his old legal pad and pen.

You might be a bit unstable emotionally, but you are certainly not stupid. And how could you not be on a mission from God? You are the only person who has ever helped me find words, and now you've done it twice. Because of you I won't live the rest of my life in a virtual prison watching Oprah and Montel between daily doses of who knows how many drugs. And now you're helping me get my wife back. You're my guardian angel, and that sounds like a mission from God if I've ever heard one.

He tried to hug me after I read the note, but I stepped back. For the first time in my life, with tears drying on my face, I didn't feel like crying anymore.

Guardian angel.

It was true. Had *always* been true; there was only one way to protect Clifford forever, and I had kept it in my breast pocket since I was six. I pulled out the over-sized lipstick tube and held it up to Clifford like a vial of antidote to every disease and poison the world had ever known.

Clifford squinted at the recorder, and offered a confused smile. He obviously had no idea what he was looking at.

"Where do you want to go, Clifford? Because wherever that is, this will keep my mother away from you. Away from Bethany too," I added.

I had meant these comments as rhetorical comforts, not really requiring a response, but Clifford immediately set pen to paper and wrote three words that filled a whole page: *PRINCE EDWARD ISLAND.*

***

I gave Clifford Mother's credit card and told him to stay out of my way for today at least, and maybe tomorrow as well. I figured he'd go to Best Buy or CompUSA and buy every program and accessory available for his Palm Pilot. He did come back to the room later with a yellow and blue plastic bag from Best Buy, but I never saw what was inside; he tucked the bag into the backpack I bought him and ignored it for the rest of the day.

His real work kept him outside until suppertime: the Corolla. That night he made a list for me of all the crap he did to that car with Mother's money (by now, even if I wanted to hide away with Clifford on this Prince Edward Island of his, Mother would send all the bloodhounds of Hell—or worse, KB—to hunt me down and lock me up for spending so much of her money) and he seemed proud of himself, but I couldn't tell much difference; the car was still beige.

Most importantly, though, this work kept him out of my hair. While he drove all over Maine searching for a lamb skin chamois and a brushless car wash, I painted a mural of sound. Since buying my iBook a year ago (Mother couldn't force herself to buy me a car, so we settled on a three-thousand dollar computer), I had converted my most valuable and interesting recordings to mp3's and saved them in the laptop. I already had over ten gigabytes of sound—nearly two thousand individual conversations and quotations from the last twelve years of my life. The files I was most interested in today were grouped together in a folder I named "Poor Clifford." I had created the folder with ironic amusement, but when I realized how *many* files I dumped in there, the name became too true to be funny. The bulk of the files starred Mother making comments either about or directly to Clifford, but many of them came from me too—mostly calling him unkind names when we were children: idiot, crack-head, butt-face, corky, gimpy, or just plain gimp. After he started getting haircuts from Bethany, I told him his hair looked like someone had eaten the raw giblets out of a frozen turkey's asshole and a box of razor blades for dessert, then barfed the whole mess on his head. I actually thought his hair looked a lot better than what Aunt Alice could with a pair of scissors, but back then I certainly couldn't have encouraged Clifford by telling him so, especially after I met Bethany and saw how much she hated me. She didn't even *know* me back then.

Of course, she knew me well enough now to have called me an unkind name of her own that I may or may not have earned. But I was crawling back to her anyway. For Clifford. For my mission. For *me*.

"Because what Mother is doing to him isn't right," I said to the empty room.

I hadn't planned to speak aloud, but now that I had, that might as well go on the CD too.

I waited until after supper to burn the disc. I wanted Clifford to be there when I added the whipped cream and cherry, so to speak. Instead of watching some crappy movie like we had done before bed each night previously, Clifford and I listened to what I had dubbed the "Mix Tape." Bless his heart, Clifford nodded and patted me on the back after the very first sound file on the disc, which was me in the motel bathroom early Monday morning: "My name is Eleanor Roberta Carlson, and *I* am on a mission from God." After that initial gesture of kindness, I suddenly panicked and almost shut off the recording; who knew how he would react to the upcoming hour of horrible words against him? But I stayed my hand. Admitting to Clifford that I hadn't always been a great cousin to him felt like part of my mission too, and I wouldn't back out now.

Clifford's eyes leaked some when Aunt Alice's spoke up from twelve years ago, "Cliff, honey, come tell your Aunt what you said your name was at the grocery store today."

Afterward, Clifford sat cross-legged on his bed and swiped at his eyes for a few minutes. He looked like a little kid again—a kid without a mommy. I had to turn away before I lost it myself.

My dry well of tears from this morning had discovered a deeper channel, it seemed, and water flowed freely there.

"What do you think?" I asked, still not facing him.

I heard four soft plastic clinks, and he stuck the Palm Pilot under my nose. One word glowed up at me: *How?*

At first I was struck by how complicated one three-letter word could be. But then I realized Clifford had ignored the truly complicated question of *why*.

Again I pulled the digital recorder from my breast pocket and held it out to him. This time he accepted it and made a quick study before handing it back. He shook his head in amazement, or maybe exasperation.

"Remember when you asked why I wear a jean jacket and I told you because heavy fabric makes me look less bony?"

His brows bunched together, but as if from an old ache rather than confusion. He remembered, alright.

"Well, Mother did say that, but that's not why I *kept* wearing jean jackets. This recorder is the newest of five. This is the first that requires no tapes. All my others are set up in your house now."

Clifford gaped.

"Not when you and Aunt Alice lived there," I assured him. "Just since Mother and I moved in." I left out that I had *wanted* to place a bug or two in his house when we were growing up, but there was no efficient way for me to replace tapes or batteries.

Now that Clifford knew my longest-kept secret, I felt foolish, like I had let an acquaintance read my diary. Which wasn't all that far from the truth, I supposed.

"Big matzo-ball," Clifford said, and grinned. He seemed pleased with himself. He picked the oddest times to open his trap.

"Let's get this thing finished up so we can mail it in the morning," I said.

The stylus clinked against the Palm Pilot for longer this time. *You tell a good story.*

"Oh," I said. "Thanks." The word tasted good, like gargling with mint mouthwash after an entire meal of garlic and salt. "Thanks a lot." I tossed my head like a pony with a new haircut. I *did* tell a good story, I realized. Unfortunately, besides Clifford and myself, only two other people would ever hear it, and one of them wouldn't appreciate my storytelling ability at all.

12

Bethany arrived Tuesday afternoon. For a moment I thought she might throw her arms around me—maybe *she* even thought she might do so—but she settled on shaking my hand in both of hers. I'd always heard about some supernatural unspoken communication women had between one another, but until this second I'd doubted such a thing existed. Bethany's big doe eyes, even behind those Buddy Holly glasses, screamed a million overlapping emotions directly into my brain, not the least of which was a huge *THANK YOU!* It was more than I could tolerate.

Then Clifford blew past me and practically tackled her in a bear hug that probably would have broken my ribs. I looked away, trying to be disgusted, but a quiet voice in my head reminded me *I* had brought her here, and that same voice guffawed and clapped that my actions had made Clifford so happy.

Suddenly I had no breath. Clifford had abandoned his beloved Bethany and now I was trapped in that same hug. My ribs didn't break after all, but my back definitely popped a few times. And I was laughing. In my surprise, that quiet voice had won over and I was *giggling* in my dumb cousin's grip. "Get off me,

Clifford, you big kumquat!" But that made him squeeze tighter and he lifted me off the ground. I heard Bethany's high laughter overlapping with Clifford's and my own. When had I laughed with other people? The sound was disturbing and wonderful.

I had to get out of there.

"Alright, you crazy buffalo, playtime's over." I tried hard to keep the giggles out of my voice, but it seemed I had tapped a hot spring of them.

For a wonder, he listened. He set me down and retreated to Bethany's side, clasping her hand. And they watched me. These grown-up Bobsie Twins stood under the concrete overhang outside our door and watched me with big dopey smiles, like I was their commanding officer and they were at attention, waiting for my orders.

"I'm not your commanding officer," I said.

They exchanged a puzzled glance, but they had to know what I was talking about, standing there watching me like that.

Bethany said, "How about we go get some supper? I just had some yogurt and a banana on the plane. I'm starving."

And now it began: I had gotten her up here to keep Clifford from mooning around the motel room like a kid whose kitten just died, and she was already taking him away. *I guess I'll just sit around here and munch on a bedspread,* I wanted to say. *You guys could bring me a mustard packet for garnish, if you can stop fawning over each other long enough to remember it.*

Instead I said, "I have a couple things to do anyway," like going to their crappy meal was the last thing I wanted to waste my time on tonight. "I'll pay for the room through the end of the week. That ought to give you time to plan out where you're going, and how you'll get there." My hot spring of laughter hadn't run so deep after all. "And I need to buy my ticket home. I'm flying out tomorrow."

Again with the glance, this time nine months pregnant. They were as bad as Clifford and Aunt Alice had been, having a whole conversation in a second of silence. Clifford drew his Palm Pilot out of his pocket and tapped at it with the stylus before handing it to me. *We want you to come too.*

Sometimes my inner dialogue was like a classroom of eager students—about thirty excuses raised their hands at once. I could call on any of them and be free of Clifford and his wife for the night.

Instead, a tornadic whimsy swept over me; I snatched the stylus from Clifford's hand and wrote a note of my own, complete with a big smiley face at the bottom: *Can we get hot dogs?*

13

I had gotten used to spending Mother's money in the last couple weeks, but I was still pleased at how low the price was for a same-day ticket from Bangor to Fort Wayne: $430 plus tax. I slapped down Mother's credit card on the airline lady's counter, anticipating Mother's praise for finding such a thrifty flight.

Then I thought of Clifford and Bethany, pulling away from here a few minutes ago in Clifford's car, free as the air itself. And I remembered one of the first recordings on the CD I sent to Mother: "Hello, Mother. I am giving Clifford back his car and coming home. He won't be back in Auburn, I'll make sure of that, but you also won't hound him anymore. And here's why..." From then on it was about the same as the CD I made for Bethany. I asked Clifford in the motel if it was wrong to blackmail your own mother, even if you were doing it for a good reason. He wrote back, *That CD is life insurance for a member of your family, not blackmail.*

Even so, I doubted there would be any praise (or the promised nose job that started this whole mess) in my future. I was lucky Mother hadn't cancelled her credit card before I could buy my ticket home.

***

The Fort Wayne International Airport isn't as impressive as it sounds. The airport itself sits on Ferguson Road and only has one hotel wrapped between its several parking lots. When I stepped out the motorized revolving doors at about two, only a few business travelers dotted the long sidewalk, and not a taxi in sight. I saw a shuttle bus with a digital readout promising a destination with Hertz, Avis, and Enterprise rental cars. I had hoped to drive home on my own, but Bethany disabused me of that idea—apparently I was seven years too young to rent a car. I wheeled my small suitcase over to a pay phone (I hadn't replaced my cell phone since bombing it against the wall at Quiznos) and looked up a taxi service in the yellow pages.

I shuddered at how Mother might respond to seeing a common taxi parked in front of her house, but I needn't have worried; she was nowhere to be found when I got home. An empty house simply *feels* a certain way, especially if it is your own. The hollow slam of the back door and the sense of waiting from the silent rooms made me instantly cold, despite my jacket. Whenever movies get as quiet as the house was, something bad usually happens, and it was too easy for me to imagine KB leaping from a closet wearing a hockey mask and holding a rusty, snarling chainsaw high above his well-groomed head.

"Stop being a prat," I told myself, or maybe I was scolding the house for freaking me out. Either way, I didn't like how thick my voice sounded, nor the way the house seemed to swallow up my voice and my breath like it was hungry for an Eleanor and denim sandwich.

"Get fragged, you mean old house," I muttered, and wheeled my suitcase out of the kitchen, up the stairs, and into my room.

Or what *used* to be my room. Everything was shredded. My room looked like a very nervous tiger had been caged there while I was away, and had used her claws (I knew it was a *her* even as the door swung open and I saw the first ribbons of clothes on the floor) to shred everything I owned. Even in the devastation

I could see her logic: she received the CD, listened to the whole thing after my brief introduction—my speech teacher at school would have called it an "attention grabber"—and set out to find the recorders. All of them.

By the end she must have been in quite a frenzy, although I doubted an observer would have seen anything but calm efficiency as she sat cross-legged on my bed and sliced my sheets, pillowcases, clothes, curtains, stuffed animals, even the lining of my mattress into narrow ribbons like colorful tapeworms, searching for tape recorders. The recordings themselves I hadn't hidden so well—piled on my ruined bed with all the strips of mattress and linen were brown-black coils of audio tape.

Again the house seemed to suck at the air around me, and the mess on the bed was a slippery pile of bowels left over from a predator's kill.

"Stop being so gosh damn melodramatic!" I yelled at the bed, and, for a wonder, it did. The house solidified around me again, and my room was just a room. "Of *course* it's just a room."

I started to unpack my remaining whole clothing. Soon I was humming, scooping the ribbons of cloth and tape off my bed and into the hall. After the humming came singing. "Papa dun preach! Ummee lumamee!" I still didn't know the words.

I giggled. It felt and sounded good in the empty room, but I missed Clifford all of a sudden. Giggling to yourself is a poor substitute for having somebody join you.

14

I had covered an exposed bedspring in the middle of the mattress with the remains of one pillow, but now I felt cold metal on my back. There was a soft, grainy sound, too, like a mouse clearing its throat.

How long had I slept? I opened one eye, trying to get my bearings. Warm yellow sunlight poured through my window. Morning then.

I was on my stomach, not my back—the bedspring couldn't be poking me in the back. And I had fallen asleep in my clothes, so how could the metal touch my skin anyway?

And what was that sound? *Churr-ip, churr-ip.* With a little imagination, it almost sounded like an animal drinking through a straw.

My sleepy mind had no trouble envisioning a giant mosquito perched on my back, hunting for a place to drink. Even the feel of cold metal on my back could be explained easily enough: a chain, of course, made of jingling keys.

I scrambled forward on the bed until I slammed into the wall. I felt the drywall give around the crown of my head, but the wallpaper held. I saw stars and heard a new sound like the

wailing of a starving kitten. After a moment I realized the sound
was coming from me. I squeezed my eyes shut again. The light
really made my head hurt.

"Oh, hold still," Mother said. Her voice carried the dim
patience she'd shown when I was a child and had sustained
minor injuries like a scraped knee or shallow splinter. She'd
said, "Oh, hold still," in that same voice as she rubbed the scrape
with peroxide or needled out the splinter.

Annoyance flared above the pain. What could she do for
a broken skull? And how was this *colossal* headache a minor
injury she could rub away?

Then came the cold metal sliding up my back and the soft
churrr-ip, churr-ip sound again.

The very top of my head throbbed, but even that was receding
into a dull ache already. I opened my eyes. The curtains were
gone, of course—that's why the room was so bright. Mother sat
on the bed behind me, making the noise. Now that I was more
awake, the *churr-ip* sound wasn't all that mystifying; scissors
through thick fabric—like denim—make that sound. And the
cold metal, now up the bottom of my neck, made sense too.

Mother was cutting off my clothes.

Even as I realized this, the scissors snicked through the
thickest part of my jacket collar, and the whole works: jacket,
shirt—even my bra!—slid forward off my back. Mother's cool
hands assisted in this process, shoving the two halves of clothes
down my arms. Those hands fell on my shoulders next and
turned me toward her. But she did not look at my face. No, she
was interested in the two halves of my jacket. First the right
half. She snipped the sleeve horizontally, all the way up the arm,
making perhaps eight thick denim loops, then cutting the loops
once more to make them into single strips. The rest of the fabric
went just as easily, Mother cutting on the seams, then in parallel
swaths. Not as quick as a paper shredder, maybe, but just as
precise. And with a big squishy blister in the web between her
right thumb and forefinger to prove she'd been at it awhile.

She was so intent on her work, I could have escaped her five times before her cool hands returned for the next half of the jacket, and who knows if she would have chased me? But I couldn't stop staring at her face. Her cheeks and forehead seemed carved from the smoothest cream cheese; her mouth was a tidy rosebud, pursed just enough to betray her concentration. But her eyes—eyes that could flay and skewer one minute, and shine golden comfort the next—were like looking through filmy windows into a vacant warehouse.

So there I sat as mother's cold scissors and cool hands disrobed the right half of my torso completely, then pulled my left leg straight out toward her, and chewed away the left, then right leg of my capris. Neither of us spoke. I suppose we each knew what the other was about—Mother the total destruction of my possessions and me hypnotized by the spectacle of it—even if we didn't know why.

She saved the left side of my jacket for last, like a little girl not eating her red Skittles until the rest were gone, because red was her favorite. She knew what she would find there, and find it she did. The scissors only scuffed and scarred the plastic edges of my digital recorder, but Mother still tried to cut it up for probably thirty seconds. The tip of one blade caught the silver "Play" button and, inexplicably, Bethany's voice sprang from the recorder's tiny speaker: "I hope this is a surprise," she said.

But that was all Bethany got out. Mother and I both stared at the little device in her palm for a moment, then she screamed like a mountain lion giving birth, a pained sound, and furious. She dropped the recorder on my bed and raised the scissors in one hand like a dagger. I wouldn't have thought it possible, but the scissors blade plunged through the oblong recorder all the way up to the grips when Mother stabbed down. She stared at the dead recorder for a moment, a satisfied half-smile dimpling one creamy cheek, but the smile faded. She pulled the recorder free of the scissors with some effort, then reached calmly for the last tatters of my shirt that still hung over my left shoulder.

My paralysis broke. I dared not fight her off while she held the scissors, but I was unsure of what she would reach for after the rest of my t-shirt lay in ribbons in her lap. My cast caught on the t-shirt's cuff as mother pulled it off, but I bent my arm behind me and jerked away from her at the same time, and was free.

Before I even knew where I was going—the irresistible desire to escape those chewing scissors ruled out any logical thought processes—I was in the front yard. The front door hung open like a mouth, giving the house a disbelieving air. I had to resist the urge to yell, "Shut your trap, you're attracting flies!" It was pretty funny, actually, imagining the house struck dumb at what had just happened inside it.

But that was over. And now the sun felt wonderful on my skin. I put my arms out and spun in the yard, soaking up the warm.

An upstairs window swung open and Mother hung her head out. "Eleanor, honey, come back inside."

Was that *pleading* in her voice? Mother had never pleaded for anything in her life. Whatever she was playing at, I wasn't biting.

"Ellie, you're not well."

Ellie? I stopped spinning. The sun turned suddenly cold and I felt goosebumps break out all over my body. My *naked* body.

In the front yard.

You're not well, Mother had said.

I had helped Clifford go AWOL without leaving an escape hatch for myself, and now I would go to Terra Haute in his place. Maybe Mother even had someone video taping this exchange right now to prove how "not well" I really was. I could see it just as clearly as if I were in front of a television watching the tape: a pale, skinny girl of eighteen barreling out of her house in nothing but a pair of pink underwear and an even pinker arm cast, spinning pirouettes in her front yard like a drunk ballerina, smiling her crazy up to the sun.

A car turned onto our street, just a few houses down, and I

slapped my arms across my chest. But I couldn't make my legs carry me back inside or even hunker down. I stood still while KB's blue and white car eased up to the curb. His lights were on and his siren gave one brief *Woo!* and then he was in front of me. He was almost my height when I didn't have shoes on. His deep-set brown eyes regarded me.

"Kendall!" Mother shouted from the window, with exactly the right amount of relief in her voice. "Thank God. I'm afraid Eleanor will hurt herself. You should see what she did to her room."

Had she known I would run outside naked if she scared me badly enough? Or was my destroyed room all the proof she had thought she would need to put me away, and this extra humiliation was just a bonus?

KB murmured, "I don't know how your mother tolerates all the crime that young people commit in this neighborhood." He grabbed my forearms and in the same motion pinned them behind my back and turned me around. I felt cold metal close around my right wrist and heard the other cuff click home around my cast. "You are under arrest for exhibiting your naked body in public."

Strange, then, that KB did not cover me up. With one strong hand on the back of my head and one at the small of my back, he ushered me into the back seat of his car. Through the cage, I saw a coarse-looking wool blanket on the front seat.

KB, still outside the car, jotted something onto a memo pad and nodded to my mother, who leaned from the window like a carving of an angel on the side of a church.

15

KB rolled down the back windows a minute or so after we pulled away from the house. Cool breeze blew across my sweaty shoulders and set my teeth chattering. The wool blanket sat unused on the front seat. "Sorry if you're cold back there. I don't want to have to hose down the back seat after you get out." Then, as if scolding a child: "You could have showered this morning."

"I'm going to eat your children with blueberries and ice cream," I told him. I doubted saying such a thing would save me from the loony bin, but at least it shut him up.

A few blocks from the station, KB pulled over. He passed the wool blanket from the front window to the back. "Cover up," he said. When I didn't move, he added, "Or don't. The point is, I gave you the option."

If KB had been staring at me through the rearview mirror, or shown *any* interest in studying my body, I would have done my best to cover up, but the truth was, he kept his eyes on the road. Also, now that my sweat had dried, the breeze felt pretty good. There was something liberating about being physically exposed to a summer day (at least, telling myself such things kept the embarrassment at bay). And besides all that, I couldn't wrap a blanket around my shoulders with my hands cuffed behind my back.

Outside the station KB covered me with the blanket himself before hauling me from the car. That monster Dwight Eisenhower towered behind the desk inside. KB had tried to make a serape out of the blanket, but it slipped down almost immediately, and I could do nothing to fix the problem. Eisenhower noticed this and hustled around the desk to cover me back up, blushing almost up to the line of his crew cut.

"Exhibitionist," KB said. He sounded defensive.

"Didn't do much to correct that, did you?" Eisenhower rumbled. The color hadn't left his face, but now I thought it was more anger than embarrassment. "And cuffs?"

KB exploded. *"When did cops who follow the rules become the* bad *cops? Huh? I am the one person in this building who doesn't flush the law down the toilet when doing so would be convenient for a friend!"* His chest puffed out like a filled hot air balloon. "Maybe if I dipped into the local honey pot more often, eh, Officer Eisenhower? Maybe if I fucked around with all the ladies in town—*then* would I be one of the good old boys? I mean, it worked for you and David Wray's daughter. Seemed like she was wet nurse to you *and* the lieutenant. One on each tit."

Eisenhower, who had two feet on KB if he had an inch, might have done murder right then and there in the foyer of the Auburn police station; the red had slid up past his hairline to paint his whole head like a cartoon character who ate a basket of hot peppers. I half expected steam to come shooting out his ears with a comical tea pot whistle. But an older man I didn't recognize came jogging out from an office back beyond the front desk. He also saw that Eisenhower was the dangerous one here. "Stand down, Dwight D," he barked.

Tendons stood out like bunches of rope in Eisenhower's bull neck, but he did as the newcomer asked, and took a step away from KB.

"Thank you, sir," KB said.

"Shut your ever-running mouth, Kendall." The newcomer's head gleamed under a few strands of black hair, as if he'd run it through a shoe buffer. "Now you listen to me, both of you. We are professionals, for God's sake, and I will not tolerate this brand of bull even one more time from either of you. Learn to work together or you will not work at all. Not here. Do I make myself clear?"

Eisenhower and KB nodded. This must be the lieutenant KB had mentioned in unflattering association with Bethany. If he'd heard the remark, he gave no indication. He turned to me. "Where in the world are your clothes, young lady?" he said, only a tad more gently than he had spoken to KB and Eisenhower.

"I don't have any," I said, which was the literal truth, I realized.

The lieutenant eyed KB and Eisenhower distrustfully. With his broad chest, potbelly, and swinging jowls, he reminded me of an upright bulldog.

KB said, "I just brought her in for exhibitionism. I will file the report immediately."

The bulldog lieutenant grunted and turned back to me. "And while he does that, Officer Eisenhower will find you some clothes." His clear, sharp eyes (the only part of his face, in fact, that did not seem to be made of pizza dough) swung upward. "Won't you Dwight D?"

"Yes, sir."

He stalked away on bowed legs, completing the bulldog illusion, and I almost giggled. Eisenhower left on his errand right away. KB stared at his back until he disappeared around a corner.

16

A month ago, I probably would have rather died than spend a night in jail. But, really, the sheets on my bunk were clean, and I had relative privacy. The only other occupied cell (out of four, total) was cattycorner from mine. A very old man snoozed on the bunk with his mouth open wide enough to accommodate Clifford's Corolla. No danger there.

I had faced my mother and come out naked and new. After staring into the empty warehouse behind Mother's eyes as she shredded my belongings with a pair of sewing scissors, I knew there was nothing left for me in Auburn.

(But her eyes hadn't been empty as she hung out the window, had they? I was done with Auburn, but maybe Auburn wasn't done with *me* yet.)

So, I slept. I had no dreams of hungry mosquitoes like living dirigibles, dragging hanks of chain made of keys thick enough to hold a ship's anchor; no drowning in sewer muck; no fear that a cold scissor blade would slide up my back and wake me. I slept the deep sleep of an adventurer. And it was good.

17

Keys rattled in my cell door. Unlike earlier this morning, when Mother had woken me up, I was not confused or scared. I knew where I was, and I sat up and stretched before greeting my visitor. "Good afternoon, Mr. Eisenhower."

He had to bend almost in half to fit through the cell door. "Morning, actually," he said. He wore a funny smile. "You've been out for about twenty hours."

Twenty hours! *Like a spelunker,* I thought giddily. "I was tired," I said.

"We received a call from one of your neighbors." He chuckled. "Edith Clemens offered to appear in court and swear on a stack of Bibles that you caused no one on the block any hurt but sympathy pains."

What was this? Was he making fun of me?

He must have seen my expression. He held up his hands, palms out. "That's not going to happen—you won't go to court."

My eyes narrowed. Sleep had dulled the hurt and humiliation of yesterday and made me docile, but I was in no mood to be mocked by this giant rhinoceros.

His funny smile finally died. "I'm supposed to take you to the museum." In Auburn, there is only one museum to speak of, so no one uses its full name. "We just have to pick up your stuff first."

"All my stuff is in ribbons," I said.

His smile returned.

Eisenhower punched a combination into a heavy metal door and excused himself for a moment. He returned with a white bundle I recognized immediately. "I don't have an iPod," I blurted out. And too bad, too. I had drooled over those things since they first came out, but they were like 300 bucks. More for the ones with more memory.

Eisenhower turned the little machine over on his palm. If he had closed his hand, the iPod would have disappeared completely. "It's got your name on it," he said innocently, and dropped it into my two cupped hands. It almost bounced off my cast onto the floor, but I caught it with my good hand.

He was right. The LCD screen read *Eleanor's Music*. "Did you—" I began. But of course he didn't. Eisenhower didn't even know me.

I followed him out to his car, clutching the iPod in a death grip against my new button-down shirt (which I thought must be one of Eisenhower's; I had rolled the sleeves to almost half their original length and they still came to my wrists). I had had an electronic box against my breast for so many years, the iPod felt like coming home, but in a good way.

Eisenhower opened the car door for me, as KB had done, but this time I sat in the front. He slid in beside me and jumped like he'd sat on a pinecone. "I knew I forgot something," he said. He dug in his pocket and pulled out a length of wire with white insulation. The wire split and led to tiny white buds—the ear phones—which I stuck in my ears. That Eisenhower might be offended at my lack of conversation never even occurred to me. He just pulled away from the station humming tunelessly to himself, still wearing that funny, satisfied smile. "Like the cat who caught the canary," I remembered Aunt Alice saying about me at Christmas when I got my first jean jacket (that little phrase had been on my very first secret recording).

Then Bethany's voice spoke through the ear buds, and I knew there would be no music. "I hope this is a surprise," she said. I shivered, remembering how Mother had screamed like a wild cat and stabbed my recorder the last time I heard those words. This time, though, Bethany was free to continue. "We didn't mean to use your voice recorder without asking, but we thought you might need a nice birthday present after you got home."

I moved the iPod off my lap to keep my tears from splashing into the control wheel.

"And Cliff was adamant that you couldn't know about the mp3 player he bought you."

Oh yes, the bag from Best Buy he'd hidden in his backpack so nonchalantly. "Clever little badger," I said aloud. Eisenhower glanced over, but said nothing.

"Hopefully you can make your way to the museum somehow to see my dad. There's also a guy named Alain there who knows somebody who might know of a job for you, if you're interested," she added hastily. She sounded almost embarrassed. "If you're not…Well, Cliff and I are working with a lawyer to get his inheritance. He said Cliff should have no problem getting it all, but we might have to wait awhile."

I had studied people's voices for over a decade—long enough to know stalling when I heard it.

"So anyway, we're moving to Prince Edward Island like Cliff's always wanted, and we could find a house with room for you too if you want." There was a long pause, and I could see her turning to Clifford with those big doe eyes wide open, broadcasting unsure excitement with enough silent volume to knock over a house. I could practically hear it through the ear buds. Present warm fuzzies aside, she and I would have some *serious* hatchet-burying to do if I shared a house with them.

"Okay, um, I guess that's it. Clifford wanted to say something but we didn't have time to—oh, okay." There were a few muffled thumps as the recorder changed hands.

Clifford held the recorder too close to his mouth. "HEATHCLIFFTON MARYBOB CARLSONIPSCHIDT!" I tore out the ear buds, but the last several syllables were plenty audible from the tiny speakers now in my lap.

"What was that?" Eisenhower asked.

I could only shrug; it was a toss up whether I was laughing harder than I was crying, or vice versa.

Two men, the older one in a suit and the younger in dirty coveralls, greeted Eisenhower and me when we pulled into the museum's gravel lot. Cicadas screeched from the tall yellow grass around the railroad tracks to our left.

The older one held out his hand. "David Wray," he said. "You must be Eleanor. I've heard a lot about you." Silence greeted this. I don't think he'd meant his statement to be as pregnant as it was. "Bethany told me what you did for Cliff and her." I stared. "Well," he said. "This is Alain," he gestured to the man in coveralls. "Did you get Bethany's letter on the what's-it?"

I nodded and patted my breast pocket, from the top of which the iPod's white and silver top peeked.

"Splendid." He waved Alain forward, looking grateful that his part was done.

Alain seemed much calmer. He reached inside his coveralls and pulled out a few stapled papers. "A friend of mine from college, Thierry Couturier, is a sound editor for a production crew in Vancouver. They're the guys who did *The X-Files*." He waited for me to fawn. I had never seen the show. "Anyway, Bethany told me about the CD you made her, and how impressed she was. I talked to Thierry, and he said if you came up he'd be willing to talk to you."

What was he ranting about? I had only graduated from high school two months ago; me getting hired by a professional sound crew because I recorded people's voices as a hobby would be like Clifford going on the road as a motivational speaker because he could say a long name that wasn't even his.

Alain must have seen my hesitation. "He's not guaranteeing anything," he said. "But if he sees promise in you, he said he could probably help you get into the Art Institute of Vancouver. That's where he got most of his crew, he said."

There was another long silence while I tried to organize all of the life-changing ideas being thrown at me. Clifford in Canada, maybe a job in Canada, maybe *college* in Canada. Mother would never visit me up there, if she ever forgave me.

But I also hoped she wouldn't chase me up there if she *didn't* forgive me. A slight hope, I supposed, but the alternative was never sleeping again.

Alain handed me the stapled papers. It was a color printout from the internet of driving directions. The trip mileage said almost 2400 miles. My eyes bugged. Twice what I had driven in pursuit of Clifford. And this time I didn't have a car or money for an airplane ticket.

"I know it's a long way for so many ifs," Alain said.

Still, I had *liked* the road. Rolling down the highway, stopping when I wanted, driving when I didn't. Windows down, hair blowing. And I'd never been west. Maybe two thousand miles wasn't that far after all.

Bethany's dad stepped forward again. "Here's mine," he said, producing his own stapled papers. "That will get you to Bethany and Cliff's hotel in Bangor. They'll be there until my lawyer gets Cliff his money. Oh!" he dug in his pocket, as Eisenhower had done in the car not ten minutes ago.

But ten minutes had already been long enough for the world to start spinning the other way, it seemed.

Mr. Wray's hand reappeared bearing a single key on a leather keychain with a metal circle bearing the Volkswagon insignia. "Happy birthday!" he yelled. His voice echoed awkwardly against the old car factory behind me. I didn't reach for the key and he shifted his weight uncomfortably. He took my good hand and wrapped my fingers around the key. He pointed. "The car is over there."

All of a sudden I knew how Clifford must have felt about his stupid Corolla when Aunt Alice bought it. The car he pointed at was angular, dark green, tiny. Love at first sight, if such a thing can be said of a car.

"Volkswagon Rabbit," Mr. Wray said. "Diesel. Fifty miles to the gallon. I suggested one of the new Biodiesel Golfs, but Bethany said Cliff insisted on the Rabbit. He said this car was made for you."

I squeezed the key in my hand until it hurt. "It's perfect," I said.

Mr. Wray finally smiled for real. "The restoration is quite good," he said. "All factory parts. Vintage Volkswagon," he boasted.

I turned to him and saw his blurry smile through more tears.

"Vintage," he repeated. "Oh, but you will have to get a new tag in thirty days. That one's temporary. No insurance, I'm afraid. But," he glanced at Eisenhower, "just be careful and you can buy insurance when you get wherever you're going."

Eisenhower seemed to be studying something in the field beyond the railroad tracks. I guessed he was pretending not to hear.

"Finally," Wray said. He looked embarrassed. "There's a hundred dollars and change in the glove compartment. It's not a lot, but it will get you fuel and maybe a campsite or two, if you sleep in your car." His cheeks were redder than Eisenhower's had been at the station yesterday.

My cast must have given the back of his head a mighty thump when I threw my arms around him. He patted my back awkwardly. "Yes, well. I'm glad you like the car." He sounded pleased.

I disengaged myself from Mr. Wray and hugged the other two in turn. My arms didn't even meet around Eisenhower's back. I was grateful he didn't squeeze.

"I'm leaving," I said. "Thank you." The words felt even better directed at strangers than when I'd said them to Clifford.

The three men nodded, each a little stunned, I think. Judging from Clifford and these guys, men were helpless and uncomfortable when faced with a crying woman. Well, I'd been uncomfortable my whole life. These guys could take my leaky eyes for a few minutes.

The Rabbit started right up with a very unrabbit-like low growl. A good sound. Driving Clifford's Corolla cross country had gotten me used to a stick shift and I was pleased that I didn't stall the car on my way out of the museum parking lot. My three new friends waved in the rearview mirror as I drove off.

A sudden panic set on me. I had no driver's license. I imagined KB pulling me over before I even got out of town and throwing me back in the cooler for driving without a license. "I'm on a mission from God," I said, and felt better.

I laid both maps on the passenger seat and studied them at a red light on Main Street. Both trips began the same way: north out of town on Interstate 69. I didn't have to decide on east or west until the Indiana Turnpike, about twenty minutes away. I found once I got there that twenty minutes hadn't been enough. I pulled onto the shoulder just before the first off ramp, leading east. The other ramp was a quarter-mile further. A quarter mile now meant a difference of over three *thousand* miles later on.

"It doesn't matter," I said. And I realized that was the truth. Neither road had any guarantees of happiness or misery, but neither was a dead end.

I gripped the leather-covered wheel with the fingers poking out of my pink cast, and set my good hand on the shifter. The Rabbit growled its pleasure at moving again.

Author's Note

Fiction readers, as a group, are well-educated people. Imagine the ten brands of expertise that ten different readers bring to a text. How about a hundred? Now imagine all that knowledge stacked up against the research and imagination of a single author. No contest! So before you come pounding on my front door to correct me in matters of American geography and antique car anatomy, let me assure you: I know there are mistakes.

I have taken liberties with the topography of Coldwater, Michigan; Bangor, Maine; and especially Auburn, Indiana (one fact in this book is that the Auburn Cord Duesenberg Museum is located in Auburn, although David Wray is not its owner). There are also flaws in my description of the Duesenberg Cliff and Bethany drive to Maine. Why wouldn't there be? If someone handed me the key to such a car I would be lucky to find the starter.

But that is what makes fiction so wonderful—a story without even one fact can still be true. I hope you shelve this book remembering the truth in it, not bitter in the knowledge that there is no Pike Street in Auburn, Indiana, or that a supercharged 1935 Model J is not among the many restored Duesenbergs at the ACD Museum. Let me make my mistakes in peace. As Bethany's dad might tell you, being gracious builds character.

André Swartley
November 26, 2004

About the Author

André Swartley (or, to telemarketers, "Andrea Snartlee") lives in northern Indiana with his wife, Kate, their cat, Linus, and their two chinchillas, Amelia and Greta. He teaches with the best damn high school English department in the country.

Printed in the United States
27059LVS00001B/61-120